The Cowboy's
Christmas Bride

By Cora Seton

Author's Note

The Cowboy's Christmas Bride is Volume 9 of the **Cowboys of Chance Creek** series, set in the fictional town of Chance Creek, Montana. To find out more about Sunshine, Cole, Ethan, Autumn and other Chance Creek inhabitants, look for the rest of the books in the series, including:

Look for the **Heroes of Chance Creek** series, too:

The SEALs of Chance Creek Series:

A SEAL's Oath
A SEAL's Vow
A SEAL's Pledge
A SEAL's Consent

Sign up for my newsletter HERE.

www.coraseton.com/sign-up-for-my-newsletter

Chapter One

"READY TO GO home?" Cole Linden reached out to stroke his fiancée's cheek.

She smiled back at him. "I think so."

Even after negotiating the chaos of Heathrow Airport at Christmas time, she was as bright and cheerful as ever. That was one of the things Cole loved about Sunshine. Her disposition resembled her name: upbeat, easygoing, happy to be alive. Sitting on a hard plastic seat, her winter coat undone, a scarf hanging every which way over her shoulders and her beautiful blond hair spilling out of a felted wool hat, she still took his breath away. After traveling around the world together for nearly three years, they probably should have been at each other's throats, but they'd hardly exchanged a cross word in all that time, which Cole counted as a miracle. The real miracle, of course, was that they'd met at all. Cole was a country boy through and through. He loved everything to do with small town living from riding horses to hunting, and he'd been running an indoor rifle range when their paths crossed. Sunshine was a city girl and a vegan—a chef who'd never set foot in a range before that fateful day.

"It'll be good to spend the holidays in Chance Creek." He couldn't wait for Christmas morning. He had a surprise for Sunshine—a big one. One that would guarantee she'd never want to leave town again. After their extended trip, he was more than ready to settle down.

"What was it you got me for Christmas again?"

Cole smiled at her none-too-subtle question. They'd been joking about presents for the past few weeks. Sunshine claimed she had a surprise that would knock his socks off, but Cole had warned her that nothing could beat what he'd gotten for her.

"Weren't you the one who said Christmas wasn't a competition? I'm sure whatever paltry gift you bought for me will be just fine. Even if it is overshadowed by my incredible present to you."

"Paltry gift? You're going to eat your words, mister." She elbowed him companionably. He kissed her on the tip of her nose. In truth, he was worried he couldn't carry off his Christmas surprise for Sunshine. It was going to take a lot of work, and he'd have to slip away almost every day once they were back in Chance Creek in order to accomplish it. That might be difficult when they were staying in a motel room and would need to share a rental car. It would have been easier if they'd been able to return to the rooms they'd once shared next to his rifle range and her café. Scott Preston inhabited them now, however. He'd been acting as their caretaker while they'd been gone, and since they were returning on such short notice, they didn't want to evict him.

Besides, it was time to hunt for a real house as soon as the holidays were over. They'd long outgrown the living quarters next to the range, and when they finally married, they'd want something more permanent.

"I don't think so. I wouldn't mind eating some of your cooking, though," Cole said to Sunshine and kissed her again. He found it hard to get enough of her. He'd been happy to be her traveling companion, but three years was an eternity to be away from the town where he'd grown up.

He was sure it was different for Sunshine. She'd only lived there for about eight months in all. She'd come to town because her aunt Cecily left her the building that housed Cole's rifle range, a tiny restaurant space and the attached living quarters. Unfortunately, Cecily had left them to Cole, too. She'd pitted them against each other in a contest to see who would ultimately win sole ownership, and at first they'd regarded each other as enemies. That didn't last once they began to share close quarters. The attraction between them was instant and electrifying, and it wasn't long before they figured out a way to share everything. Cole continued to run the rifle range and manage the apartment buildings he owned. Sunshine ran her café from the restaurant space. They lived together in the attached rooms.

But several months later, when they became engaged, they'd received another message from their attorney. It seemed that Cecily's will had a secret codicil to be read only if Sunshine and Cole decided to marry. The old woman had left them each a large sum of money. As soon as Cole found out about it, he knew what they needed to do. Sunshine had always talked about traveling the world. Here was their chance. He'd paid off the mortgage on the two apartment buildings, which freed up funds to pay Scott a salary to run them and the range while they were away. Scott had moved into their rooms beside the restaurant to keep an eye on things, and Cole and Sunshine had embarked on an epic journey, the likes of which Cole had never imagined taking.

"I can't wait until I have a kitchen to call my own again," Sunshine said. She peeled off her hat and scarf, and struggled out of her coat. Cole helped her drape them over her chair.

He'd determined at the start to let Sunshine call the shots about the itinerary and duration of the trip. This was her chance to study cooking in the field, so to speak, and learn from experts in all kinds of situations. He found it easy to be patient. For one thing, he was head over heels in love with Sunshine, for all their talk about a long engagement. For another, Sunshine had assured him that when they were done they'd return to the town he dearly loved. That was a huge concession from a city girl, and he wanted to honor the spirit in which she made it by throwing himself into the adventure wholeheartedly.

He'd never guessed she'd make the trip so long, though. He'd begun to think they'd never get home.

Still, he was proud of Sunshine and the way she'd handled the rigors of so much travel. They hadn't stuck to tourist destinations; far from it. Sunshine was fascinated by indigenous recipes, and in every country they visited, she took them off the beaten track into villages and hamlets and somehow convinced women—and men—to teach her everything they knew about cooking. Cole had done his best to photograph the locales, people, ingredients and food preparation steps. They'd taken copious notes in order to correlate recipes, photographs and information about people and locations. When they got home,

Sunshine hoped to combine them into a cook-book and get a publishing deal.

Cole had watched people all around the world take to Sunshine. He wasn't sure if it was her smile, her laugh, or the shimmer of her blond hair that caught their attention and made them go out of their way for her, but he couldn't count the number of kindnesses complete strangers had performed for them during the past three years.

He'd worried that such an intense journey might cause trouble between them, but the more they traveled, the more he loved Sunshine. With Christmas looming and their return home at hand, he'd decided to give her the one other thing he knew she wanted: a restaurant. He'd purchased one already, sight unseen, from a realtor he knew and trusted back in Chance Creek. It was located in the heart of town and he figured Sunshine could make it a success.

"That snow doesn't look promising," Sunshine said, glancing out of the airport window where a cold afternoon had long since faded into darkness. "I think it's coming down even harder."

"I'm sure it'll be fine."

She nodded. "I hope so." Fidgeting in her seat, she added, "We're not due to board for another half hour. Want to go for a little walk?"

"If we stand up now, we'll lose our seats." The waiting room was packed with travelers.

Cole was thankful they'd gotten tickets at all since they'd bought them with only a couple weeks' notice.

"You're right," she admitted with a sigh. "I hope I can sleep on the plane. It's a long flight."

He doubted he would. He was too wired thinking about all he needed to do in the next ten days. Collect the paperwork and keys for the restaurant, hire contractors, rip out anything that needed repairs. He knew it was unlikely he'd get everything done before Christmas, but he wanted to make the restaurant look its best before he presented it to Sunshine. He took her hand. "It's going to be busy when we get home. I'll probably have to spend a lot of time at the rentals." Best to lay the groundwork for his disappearances now.

"You don't think Scott's doing a good job?"

"I'm sure he is, but he's not the owner."

"Of course. I have a lot of shopping to do anyway. I need to throw packages together fast for my family and get them in the mail."

"I guess we'll both be busy, then." Cole was relieved. It was crucial his present remained a surprise: that's what made it so much fun. If Sunshine was busy, she wouldn't ask difficult questions—or have time to pry. Last year she'd found his gift three days before Christmas. Refusing to admit defeat, he'd had to rush out and find a replacement present. He reached over to take her hand and frowned. Sunshine suddenly looked a little pale. "You feeling all right?"

"All the travel is catching up to me, I think."

"It'll be good to be home."

"You've got that right."

SUNSHINE SHIFTED IN her uncomfortable chair again. Pregnant. She was pregnant. For the last four weeks Sunshine hadn't been able to think of anything else. She was thrilled and terrified and so confused she didn't know which way she was heading most of the time. When Cole announced he'd be busy with the rental complex once they got home, she breathed a sigh of relief. Her pregnancy wasn't her only secret; the ranch she'd bought for Cole was another big surprise.

She'd bought it on an impulse only days after she'd realized she'd missed her period. First she'd had to confirm her pregnancy without letting Cole know. She'd gone out of her mind with impatience until Cole had wandered off one afternoon to visit an agricultural museum outside of London. Then she'd rushed to the closest pharmacy, bought an over-the-counter pregnancy test, taken it in a public restroom... and tossed the evidence in the trash as soon as she'd snapped a photograph of the results.

Pregnant.

Sunshine hadn't known whether to laugh or cry. She'd been struggling for months to decide what to do about her future. Now the question had been answered for her. Forget about opening a restaurant. It was time to buy a home. She'd called a realtor she knew in Chance Creek, told her what she wanted and was thrilled when the realtor said she had one that would fit the bill. "I'll take it," she'd said after looking at the photos online; she knew ranches were hard to come by and she didn't want to risk losing the place and the chance to give Cole a fabulous Christmas present. In the rush to sew up the deal she'd had no time for second thoughts.

Now—after she'd put her money down on the ranch—she'd succumbed to doubts again. On the one hand, she couldn't wait to be a mother and she adored Cole. She'd enjoyed living in Chance Creek far more than she'd expected to during the months she'd stayed there.

On the other hand, her ambitions would be difficult to pursue in a small Montana town. She was a vegan chef, for heaven's sake. How could she take the world by storm in cowboy country?

It made far more sense to return to Chicago where she'd once helped to run a highly success-ful restaurant. If she sold the ranch she'd just bought, she could put a hefty down payment on a restaurant and build a real business.

Unfortunately, she couldn't picture Cole happy in Chicago. He was a country boy through and through. He had definite thoughts about the kind of home he wanted to raise their children in, too. He wanted them to have lots of space to run and play and he wanted them to grow up on a property that they could take over one day.

In other words, he wanted a ranch.

And thanks to the help of her realtor, she'd found him one. Everything was signed, sealed and delivered.

She couldn't change course now.

She squeezed Cole's hand and he squeezed hers back, his expression full of tenderness. She had to smile when she pictured his reaction on Christmas morning when she took him out to show it to him. Of course, between now and then it needed a lot of spiffing up. She hoped she could get at least some of that done before Christmas.

And if she had to put off her dream of one day owning a real restaurant—not just a hole in the wall café like the one attached to the rifle range—well, she was sure it would happen someday. Until then she'd make do.

She glanced at Cole again, studying the handsome man who had become so crucial to her happiness. She remembered when she first arrived in Chance Creek. She'd been aghast to find the building she'd inherited already inhabited by an uncouth cowboy with a penchant for firearms.

Soon enough she'd fallen for Cole hook, line and sinker, and they'd had so much fun during those first months after they'd buried the hatchet and learned to work together. Cole had ruled the roost at his indoor rifle range and she'd cooked for his clients and anyone else who'd ventured into the neighborhood. When customers were scarce, they'd fooled around. She found it hard to keep her hands off of the man.

Three years abroad hadn't changed that. Cole could set her nerves alight with a single touch. Every night when they slid into bed she felt like she had the first time they'd been together. His body gave her endless pleasure. What more could she ask for?

She pressed her hand to her belly, tingling with the knowledge that her baby was growing inside of her.

Their baby.

It was such a precious secret. A secret it had been killing her to keep. Every time Cole made love to her she'd wanted to scream it out loud.

But she had to wait just a little longer. She sighed and leaned against Cole's shoulder.

And noticed the woman heading straight for them.

"COLE LINDEN, IS that you?"

The strident female voice startled Cole—and several people around him. He looked up to see a redhead approaching him just as the man in the seat next to him stood up, collected his things and walked away.

A familiar redhead…

"For God's sake, it's Frannie Lake—don't tell me you don't remember your first kiss!" the woman exclaimed.

Cole glanced at Sunshine, hoping she wasn't paying attention, but unfortunately she was. "Of course I remember you, Fran. Good to see you." It wasn't good, though. Fran was halfway right; she hadn't been his first kiss, but she'd been his first in other ways and he remembered her all too well. He hoped like hell she'd grown up in the intervening years.

"What are you doing at Heathrow?"

"Heading home." He hoped Fran read his disinclination to talk in his tone, but she didn't—or she ignored it. Plopping down in the empty seat beside him, she sighed. "Me, too."

"To Oklahoma?" He was about to tell her she was at the wrong gate.

"No, silly. To Chance Creek. My folks are still there. We all come home at Christmas. You know that."

Cole had always done his best to avoid her. She'd been a little hard to get rid of back in high school. "Say hello to your folks for me when you get there." He lifted the magazine he'd bought for the plane ride to signal the end of the conversation.

"You'll have to stop by and say it yourself. I'll make sure Mom hangs the mistletoe and you can give me another kiss. I've missed them. Nobody kisses like a Chance Creek cowboy."

Cole cleared his throat. Fran didn't seem quite herself and Sunshine didn't look at all happy. "Um… Fran, this is my fiancée, Sunshine Patterson. Sunshine, meet Fran. We knew each other as kids."

"In the biblical sense." Fran elbowed Cole. "He's a humdinger, isn't he? Whew, he used to ride me hard and put me up wet." She laughed long and hard at her joke, then seemed to notice she was the only one who did. "Fiancée, did you say? Lord, here I am making an ass out of myself. I've had my pre-flight drink already. Hate airplanes, you know? They scare me stiff. Please ignore everything I just said." She leaned around Cole to shake Sunshine's hand. "Besides, if you're his fiancée, you know exactly what I mean."

Sunshine snatched her hand back. Cole stood up. "Sunshine, how about me and you go get a snack?"

"They're going to call our flight in a minute."

"Oh, we won't be going anywhere for ages," Fran said. "Look at that snow. We'll be lucky to fly out tonight. Heck, I'll probably sober up and need to get drunk all over again. You all can join me."

"I don't think so." Sunshine's normally bubbly demeanor was as cold as ice.

But Fran didn't seem to notice. "Do you remember that camping trip we took?" She laughed as Cole slowly sat down again, a braying sound that had more heads turning. She leaned forward to catch Sunshine's eye. "He promised my parents it was a group trip and that the girls would sleep in one tent and the boys in another. Had me fooled. We got out into the wilderness and guess what? There was me and him and a single sleeping bag. I'm not sure we left the tent the whole weekend."

"Fran, do you mind?" Cole couldn't believe what she was saying.

"Shit, am I doing it again? I'll be good, I promise." She pretended to zip her mouth closed, then immediately laughed her braying laugh again. "Don't worry, Cole. A girl like Sunshine knows that a guy like you comes with a past. Right, honey? I mean, Cole's no boy scout. Anyone could see that."

Cole scanned the waiting area, looking for any seats to shift to, but it was standing room only. Just as he turned to Sunshine again, the loudspeaker crackled and a flight attendant came on.

"If I may have your attention, this announcement is in reference to flight one zero one nine to New York City. I'm sorry to tell you that our departure time has been delayed until seven-thirty. Our approximate boarding time will be an hour from now."

Groans followed the announcement and Cole's shoulders tightened. "We need to eat." He cut off Fran before she could start in again.

Sunshine nodded. "We still can't leave the chairs, though."

Cole thought fast. Normally, he'd volunteer to go and fetch something, but there was no way he'd leave Sunshine with Fran. "I'll fight off anyone who tries to sit down."

Sunshine looked like she wanted to object, but instead she nodded. "Fine. What would you like?"

Cole nearly asked for a burger, but remembered just in time that might be the final straw for his vegan fiancée. "Whatever you can find." He tried to grab her hand and give it a commis-erating squeeze, but she stood up and he missed. She left without another word, winding through the crowd. Cole plunked his carry-on bag into her vacant seat and glared at a man who'd immediately started toward it.

"She's pretty. You always did have good taste." Fran put a hand on Cole's knee. Cole swatted it away.

He wished that was true.

SUNSHINE STEADIED HERSELF against a wave of dizziness. She must have stood up too fast. Or else it was the anger which had flooded her body since Fran had opened her mouth. Sunshine knew Cole had slept with other women before her; he'd been twenty-nine when she'd met him, and like Fran said, he was no boy scout. That didn't mean she enjoyed meeting his former conquests. Certainly not someone like Fran who wanted to share all the details.

Had Cole really slept with a woman like that?

She consoled herself that he'd probably been a randy teenager at the time, getting away with whatever he could. It must not have meant much if they hadn't stayed together.

Or had Fran left Cole in the dust? Her suit, heels, and slick carry-on bag proclaimed she was a frequent traveler, despite her evident fear of flying. Maybe she'd outgrown Cole and figured Sunshine was a country bumpkin ripe for teasing.

The idea left her seething.

So did the fact Cole had decided to stay in his seat and send her to fetch the food. Hardly the gentleman-like thing to do.

On the other hand, she knew he'd wanted to spare her more of Fran's stories. Was that gentlemanly? Possibly. He'd regain some lost ground if Fran wasn't there when Sunshine got back.

She stalked through the terminal until she reached a food court. It would be difficult to find anything truly vegan here, and in the end she settled for a fruit cup and a muffin that had seen better days. She knew Cole wanted a burger, but she wouldn't pander to his murderous proclivities. Not today. She got him a vegetable wrap and a peach smoothie.

That oughta teach him.

By the time she made it back to the gate, she was starving and lightheaded. Deciding she was probably dehydrated, she made a U-turn and picked up several bottles of water at a kiosk.

Fran must have left by now, she consoled herself, but when she approached the gate, she saw Cole and Fran deep in conversation. Fran's hand rested on Cole's knee and he was doing nothing to move it. Instead, he listened to what she had to say with rapt attention.

Sunshine stopped in her tracks.

Unsure whether to continue or backtrack, she could only watch as Fran reached up with her other hand and brushed something from Cole's cheek. The gesture was so intimate it shocked Sunshine to the core.

Cole turned, caught sight of her and pulled back from Fran in alarm. "Sunshine." He stood up.

There was nothing for it but to continue forward. Fran smirked as she approached and fury swept through Sunshine again. The woman knew exactly what she was doing. She was trying to cause trouble.

"Your dinner." She shoved the veggie wrap and smoothie into Cole's hands and took her seat, ignoring Fran.

"Looks… good," Cole said.

"Well, I'm going to try to get some shut-eye, seeing as we aren't leaving for three hours," Fran said.

"Three hours?" Sunshine couldn't believe it. "I thought they said one."

"It got delayed again," Cole informed her.

"Great."

"It was wonderful talking over old times with you, Cole. Can't wait to have you over for dinner," Fran said and curled up in her chair, giving Sunshine a wink before she closed her eyes.

"It's not what you think," Cole mumbled, leaning close.

"Are you sure?" She took a bite of her muffin and nearly spit it out again. It tasted like cardboard. Cole looked about as unhappy as she felt as he examined his wrap.

"We dated in high school. That's it. She was

telling me about her parents. Sounds like her dad isn't doing too well—"

"Whatever."

She couldn't wait to get on the plane and get out of here.

Chapter Two

C OLE DIDN'T THINK he'd ever been so happy to arrive at a cheap motel. The Big Sky was about as nondescript as they came. A two-story building, its parking lot was plowed, with mounds of snow circling it like a stockade. It felt so familiar—and at the same time so foreign, like something he'd seen in another life. He guessed he'd been away too long.

The sun was fading away behind bleak, gray clouds, the sky echoing the leaden feeling that had lodged in his heart. In the end, their flight hadn't taken off until seven o'clock in the morning. Fran had woken up again all too soon in her uncomfortable seat at the gate, and hadn't shut up about their high school days for hours.

Sunshine had grown silent, simmering with what looked like rage. He hadn't seen her so angry since the first few days of their acquaintance. He wanted to muzzle Fran, and considered raising his voice at her, but with the waiting room so crowded he didn't want to make a scene—or worse, get them kicked out of the airport. He also felt sorry for the woman; Fran's father had received bad news and Fran was masking her fear and sorrow with alcohol. Her dad, who'd been treated for stage-two colon cancer, had found out he would need to undergo another operation, followed by chemotherapy. Fran had been telling him about the prognosis when Sunshine reappeared from buying them dinner. He'd also gleaned that Fran had gone through a divorce a year and a half ago. She wasn't in a good place.

He wanted to explain all of that to Sunshine, but she'd been too put off by Fran's behavior to listen. He couldn't blame her. Fran was acting out and making a nuisance of herself, and worse—she kept touching him. He was more than a little relieved when their flight finally took off and Fran was seated nowhere near them.

They'd boarded different planes in New York and they hadn't seen Fran again. Cole had finally relaxed, but Sunshine hadn't lightened up, even when he tried to make a joke about the whole thing. When he ventured forth on another explanation, she turned her back on him and told him she didn't want to hear it.

What a way to arrive home, Cole thought with a sigh. But home they were—at last.

He certainly felt like a world traveler now. He

could boast that he'd set foot on six out of the seven continents and Sunshine could say she'd cooked on them, too. Cole had been impressed with the way Sunshine adapted to sleeping in huts in the Andes, on pontoon boats in Southeast Asia, and in yurts in Mongolia. Her stamina put his to the test as they explored the furthest nooks and crannies of the world.

But Sunshine had tired of rustic living after the first year. A city girl born and bred, she then took Cole on an expansive tour of the cities of Europe and Asia. A tour that lasted nearly two years.

When their trip stretched on and on, Cole ached for the open skies and broad expanses of the country, but Sunshine became more citified with each metropolis they visited. As her heels grew higher and her makeup more expensive, she exchanged the handwoven leather and bead bracelets she'd been given by villagers for diamond earrings and necklaces bought on the main shopping strips of Paris and Rome. Cole began to wonder if he'd ever known Sunshine at all.

But she'd remained cheerful and excited through it all.

Until now.

Cole glanced at her again. She'd sat in an exhausted stupor through the last flight. Cole had found it equally hard to sleep, and even when he dozed he had woken frequently when the plane encountered turbulence.

Now it was almost dinner time again. She leaned back against the seat with her eyes closed, but he couldn't tell if she was sleeping. He reached over and put a hand on Sunshine's shoulder. "We're here."

She opened her eyes, took in the drab facade of the motel and nodded. Without a word she undid her seatbelt, gathered her purse and stepped out. Cole joined her, taking in her ridiculous but beautiful high-heeled leather boots. She'd likely break her neck on the ice before they reached the front entrance. When he went to take her arm, Sunshine smiled at him, but that didn't dispel the tiredness that etched her face. He needed to get her to their room, fast.

They walked in silence to the lobby where a woman greeted them with a frown. "Sorry, folks. We're full up, just like the sign says."

"We have a reservation," Cole said. "Under the name Linden."

The woman was already shaking her head. "Like I said, we're full up. Everyone's already checked in."

"We have a reservation." He couldn't keep the steel from his tone. "Look it up."

"Okay, Mr. Linden." She typed into her computer and shrugged. "I'm sorry. Just like I said."

Cole braced his hands on the counter. "We have to be in there. We're a little late, but—"

She pursed her lips and typed some more. "You're more than a little late, Mr. Linden. Your reservation started last night."

"We got held up at the airport."

"It's a shame you didn't let us know. We could have held your room. Instead we gave it to someone else."

Anger boiled up inside Cole. "Like hell. I reserved that room for two weeks!"

"And you didn't show up or notify us of your change in plans. We didn't charge you." The woman shrugged again.

"I don't care if you didn't! I need a room—now!"

"Cole." Sunshine's voice held a warning.

The woman folded her arms over her chest. "We're fully booked, Mr. Linden. I think you'll find most places are. You might try Billings—"

"I'm not driving two hours to find a motel."

"Cole," Sunshine said again. "You're not helping."

He clamped down on the urge to swear. She was right. Guilt swamped him again at the unhappy expression on his fiancée's face.

"Isn't there someone you know?" she asked.

He'd never seen her so pale and drained, even in the deepest jungle or on the most forbidding mountain. Maybe Sunshine was getting ill. If so, he couldn't waste time arguing.

"Take a seat," he told her and waved at the armchairs positioned by the window. "I'll find us somewhere to go."

IF SHE HAD to wait another minute to go to bed, she was going to be sick, Sunshine thought. This pregnancy stuff wasn't for the faint at heart. Not after hours and hours of listening to another woman flirt with her fiancé.

She couldn't believe Cole hadn't shut Fran down. She understood he didn't want to make a scene, but surely there was something he could have said to make her stop. On some level, Cole must have enjoyed being flanked by two women, one his fiancée, the other obviously wanting some kind of relationship. She couldn't believe he'd promised to stop by and say hello to Fran's folks. Didn't he know he was encouraging her?

Or was that his plan?

She watched Cole pace the small lobby with his phone pressed to his ear and prayed he'd find them a place to go. She had to get out of these stupid high-heeled boots.

She tried to distract herself by making lists of all the things she'd need to do at the ranch before she showed it to Cole, but the fun had gone out of the game. Every time she thought about Christmas morning, she thought about

Fran saying, "We'd love to have you join us for dinner some night." If he actually tried to go she'd have to slug him.

And she didn't believe in violence.

Fran certainly wasn't the first woman to make a play for Cole since Sunshine had dated him. It used to be funny, but now she was pregnant, it took things to a whole new level. Maybe she'd feel differently if she and Cole were already married. As it was, she felt too vulnerable. It was one thing to decide to put her career on hold while she raised a child with Cole. It was another thing altogether to end up a single mother while Cole reunited with his childhood love.

Sunshine sighed. She didn't really think Cole would leave her. She was letting her imagination run away with her because she was worried about the future. Given the circumstances, it was easy to feel like her choices had been taken away from her. She hadn't ever made concrete plans around parenthood, mostly because she'd never seen herself as a full-time stay-at-home mom. On the other hand, Cole had made it very clear during this last portion of their trip he thought children belonged with their parents, rather than with the nannies that seemed ever-present in London. All the questions that swirled in her mind only served to make her feel worse.

"You won't believe this," Cole said, slipping

his phone back into his pants pocket. "Ethan Cruz is married."

"To Lacey?" Sunshine had never actually spoken to the woman, but she remembered all the talk that swirled around Ethan's spoiled-rotten fiancée.

"No. Apparently Lacey broke off their engagement, got engaged to someone else, broke that off too and now she's gone back to college to get her degree."

"Wow. Busy girl."

"Anyway, Ethan met someone new. Her name's Autumn. She helped him turn his parents' house into a Bed and Breakfast, so they actually have a guest room for us."

Sunshine brightened a little. That sounded promising. "Does it have a private bath?"

"It does."

"Thank God. I need a hot soak more than anything."

"I'll get you there in a jiffy."

Sunshine softened. Cole always looked out for her. Surely together they'd find a way so she could balance motherhood with her career. It was time to put Fran out of her mind, too. She knew Cole; he was polite to a fault with most women. He probably just didn't know how to get her to stop when she'd rambled on and on back at the airport. Standing up, she swayed for a moment. Cole put out a hand to steady her. His touch was gentle, and Sunshine relaxed into it. "Lead the way."

Cole did so. They drove in silence the short distance to the Cruz ranch and Sunshine was more relieved than she could say to arrive. Autumn Cruz, a petite woman with light brown hair and blue eyes, threw open the front door and invited them in. Ethan appeared behind her as they entered and pulled Cole into a rough hug.

"I thought you'd never come home!"

"I thought I might never get the chance." Cole shot Sunshine a look and backtracked. "I mean, we were having a good time…"

Sunshine frowned. She'd known Cole was anxious to get home these last few months, but he'd never complained about seeing the trip through. To her way of thinking it had made no sense to cut it short; they'd had a once-in-a-lifetime chance to travel and they might as well make the best of it.

Still, perhaps three years *was* excessive.

"Let me show you your room. You have to be exhausted," Autumn said, leading the way into a great room with floor-to-ceiling windows that made the most of the view. Upstairs were a number of bedrooms, including one whose door was propped open. They entered to find a queen-sized bed, dresser and desk, an en suite bathroom with an enormous soaker tub, and more views out of the windows.

"Normally I'd say I'm fine," Sunshine told her, "but today I can't summon the strength. I need a soak and sleep."

"Of course. I'll bring up a tray of snacks in a minute to tide you over until morning. I wish I didn't have to kick you out so soon." Sunshine looked at her blankly and Autumn's face fell. "I assumed Cole had told you; I've got more guests coming tomorrow afternoon. I'll need the room back by lunch time."

"Oh, of course," Sunshine said, her spirits dipping again. "We'll find somewhere else to stay."

"Don't worry," Autumn assured her. "Claire and Jamie have room for you tomorrow night. Do you remember Jamie?"

"Jamie Lassiter? Of course! He's married, too?" She remembered the easygoing cowboy who used to work for Ethan's family. He used to hang out at the rifle range with the others.

"That he is. To Ethan's sister, Claire."

"I never met her."

"You'll like her. She's an interior decorator. They have a baby named Lynn. Anyway, Jamie would love to catch up with Cole, so it's all settled."

Soon after she left, Cole brought up their bags and Sunshine sat on the bed, exhausted and thoroughly disheartened from the news they'd have to leave in the morning.

"Guess there's no use unpacking," Cole said.

"No, not if we're leaving tomorrow. Mind if I hog the tub?"

"Can I join you?"

Sunshine shook her head. "Not tonight." When his face fell, she went on. "I'm sorry. I don't feel very well. Any other time." They had bathed that way so many times in the past; she hoped he didn't mind that she was refusing, but after all Fran's stories about their many encounters, she just didn't think she could be with him that way right now.

Cole's expression tightened as if he could hear her thoughts, but he didn't protest. "Anything I can get you?"

"No. I just need peace and quiet. And sleep. I'll keep my bath short."

"Take as long as you want." He came to drop a kiss on her head. "I'll go catch up with Ethan."

"I'll see you later." She bent down to open a suitcase and look for her robe, breathing a sigh of relief when the door shut behind Cole. The memory of Fran's stupid stories was only one reason she didn't want to bathe with Cole. She was afraid he would recognize the early signs of pregnancy she'd begun to see in her body. Her breasts were just a little bigger, for one thing. The twinges she felt deep in her abdomen weren't visible, of course, but Cole knew her so well— wouldn't he sense something was going on?

She scooped her robe out of the suitcase, hurried into the en suite and locked the door. Turning on the taps, she let the water run into the tub and began to strip off her clothes.

Before she traveled, she hadn't thought much about children, but unexpectedly, children had figured into her trip right from the start. She'd wanted to learn about cooking methods all over the world and she'd found it easy to meet people in the various countries she traveled to who were eager to invite her into their homes and demonstrate their techniques. She'd expected to spend time with women as they cooked over their fires, hearths, grills and stoves, but she'd never realized that meant she'd spend time with their kids, too. Looking back, it should have been obvious, but as a single woman with no nieces or nephews, children hadn't crossed her mind. She'd hardly spent any time with them since she was one herself, but all over the world babies, toddlers, preschoolers and even school-aged kids had surrounded Sunshine as she watched their mothers prepare meals.

At first she'd been somewhat awkward around the little ones, but as time went by she began to enjoy their company. She worked hard to make them laugh—which actually hadn't been that hard. As she warmed up to the children, their mothers warmed up to her, until Sunshine realized she'd been missing something in her life at home.

During the first year, as they traveled through many remote regions, she engaged with one large family after another, surrounded by women and children of all ages. Even when she moved on to the larger centers in Europe, she still encountered children in many of the kitchens she visited.

It must have worked some magic on her birth control. Sunshine had never missed a day of taking the Pill—she was sure of it.

Mostly.

There was that time she'd gotten ill in Cambodia. And the time they'd been delayed in the hills of India and hadn't made it back to the city to a drug store before her old set ran out. But they'd been careful then. And once they returned to Europe they'd always been in reach of a prescription.

She couldn't be pregnant now.

But somehow she was.

When Sunshine had learned the news, joy had swelled her heart to bursting, but then reason kicked in and she'd become terrified. Those two emotions had been at war within her ever since. Her arms ached to hold her baby, but she was afraid she'd be a lousy mother. Whenever Cole wasn't looking, she read everything she could about pregnancy on her cell phone. She hadn't succumbed to more than passing nausea yet, but the past twenty-four hours had worn her down to the bone.

What would Cole say when he knew?

She knew the answer: they had to get married. They had to buy a house. They needed a permanent home.

When she showed him the ranch, he'd be thrilled.

She hoped.

Sometimes when she woke up in the wee hours of the morning and couldn't fall asleep again, she wondered if she'd got it all wrong. What if Cole didn't want children after all? What if he was sick of her after nearly three years on the road?

What if Fran looked all too enticing after a monotonous diet of Sunshine?

That was just the exhaustion talking, Sunshine told herself. She shut off the taps and stepped into the blessedly hot water. Sinking down into it, she let the heat drain some of the stress out of her muscles. Maybe she could buy a tub like this one for their new house. That would be heaven.

Once again the vision of an ultra-modern Chicago restaurant paraded through her mind. There was still time for her to sell the ranch and insist they move to the city—

But Sunshine knew she couldn't do that to Cole—or her unborn baby. She'd create a haven for her family while Cole tried his hand at ranching the way he'd always wanted. She'd be happy.

It was time to settle down.

COLE WASN'T A man to create trouble out of nothing, but it worried him that Sunshine had turned down his offer to share her bath.

It was all Fran's fault, too. Lord, that woman had a mouth. When they were teens he'd ignored that aspect of her personality, too enthralled by her other attributes. Once he'd spent a few months in her company, though, even those attributes hadn't been compensation enough for the fact they had nothing in common. Fran was all about appearances and one-upmanship. She'd left Chance Creek, become an insurance agent and fought her way up the corporate ladder until she could flash her lavish lifestyle around whenever she came home to visit her folks.

Cole hoped Sunshine would soon forget all about her in the festive activities to come. He'd make sure the two women didn't cross paths again—even if he did check on Fran's father over the weekend—and soon enough Fran would leave town again. She never stayed long.

For the moment, he'd let Sunshine have a good soak alone, as much as he wanted to be there to hold her. When she'd had a chance to rest, they'd reconnect. Soon enough they'd laugh about this. He bundled up and went outside to look for Ethan.

"Cole! Over here," Ethan called out when Cole came around the side of the house. "Just heading to the barn to do a few chores. Want to come along?"

"Sure thing." Stuffing his gloved hands into the pockets of his winter coat, he hurried to catch up to Ethan. A minute later he stepped into the barn and took a deep breath. Now this was what country should smell like. He inhaled again.

"You've been away too long, haven't you?"

"Damn straight. Thought I might never make it back."

"You said that before." Ethan tilted his hat back. "Something happen while you were gone?"

"Sunshine remembered she's a city girl." He gave a quick rundown of their travel itinerary.

Ethan whistled. "You think she still wants to live in Chance Creek?"

"I sure hope so. I don't want to live in Chicago."

"Does she miss her family?"

Cole felt a pang. "Probably. Although her parents visited us in Paris a couple of months ago."

"Still. Women like to live near their kin."

Cole followed Ethan around as he tended to his chores. He itched to pitch in, but Ethan moved with the practical grace of a man on his own turf.

"Going to take over the rifle range again?"

"I'm thinking of heading in a new direction." Cole pretended to examine the tools that hung from pegs along the wall. In the past, he'd run the range more as a way to honor his father's memory than because it really called to him. It wasn't a huge money-making operation. Now that they were home, he needed to think long term.

"Really? Like what?"

"I don't know. Ranching, maybe?" Buying the restaurant had eaten a big hole into his savings, but he thought he might still be able to swing a down payment on a ranch. A small one. Especially if he sold his rentals.

"Huh. You got a partner?" Ethan kept working.

"Nah. Figured I'd start on my own."

"Well, I'm not one to interfere, but I wouldn't do it that way. It's hard work, and I don't think Sunshine will be a lot of help. Nothing against Sunshine, she's great—but like you said, she's not a country girl."

"No. I thought I'd start with a small herd. Go from there."

Ethan was already shaking his head. "You won't make any money. It's go big or go home these days, Cole. The business ain't what it used to be. That's why we've got the guest house and three other partners pitching in to pay the bills."

Cole's shoulders slumped. He'd halfway known that already, but he would have liked to find out he was wrong. "What would you do if you were me?"

Ethan rubbed the back of his neck. "I don't rightly know. Something specialized, that's for sure. You should talk to Jamie. He's got an idea a minute. He's turned his horse breeding business into a going concern."

"I'll do that." Cole looked his friend over while Ethan bent over his task. "Ranching suits you. I was sorry to hear about your folks, though." Before he'd come outside, Autumn had filled him in about the accident that claimed Ethan's parents' lives.

Ethan nodded. "It was hard going after Mom and Dad passed away. For a while I thought I would lose everything—especially when Lacey ditched me. Turned out to be a blessing in disguise, though. I met Autumn and everything turned around. I love being a dad. Arianna might only be twenty-one months, but that girl has got me wrapped around her finger. And can you keep a secret?"

"Sure." Why not? He was already keeping a big one.

"Autumn's pregnant again. She's due next summer."

"That's great." He hoped he sounded enthusiastic. He was happy for Ethan, but he was jealous, too. He wanted everything Ethan had. A ranch, a home, a wife, a family.

"Something wrong?" Ethan asked.

Cole looked up to find his friend watching him. "Nope. Just wondering when it'll be my turn."

"You and Sunshine didn't marry while you were gone? We all wondered if you would pick some exotic location for your wedding."

Cole sighed. "No, we wanted to wait until we got home." It seemed like an oversight now. "We'll nail down our plans soon."

"What are you getting her for Christmas?"

"It's a secret."

"I won't tell." Ethan looked interested. "Shoot."

"I bought Sunshine a restaurant in town. She needs something to ground her here—besides me—and she's such a good chef, it seemed only fair to get her one since she's agreed to live here rather than return to Chicago."

"That sounds like a great idea."

"It did when we were in Europe. Now I'm not so sure. Do you think there's too much competition in town?"

"Nah. People like to eat."

"I have a lot of work to do on it before Christmas."

"Tell me how I can help. I keep pretty busy, but I can always find an hour or two in my day if I look for them, and I'm pretty handy." Ethan turned back to his chores. Cole followed along.

"Normally I don't like to be indebted to other people, but I'll take you up on that offer. There's too much for one man to do in the time that's left."

"Call me anytime."

"Thanks." When Ethan was done, he followed him back to the house, feeling more hopeful than he had an hour ago. He'd missed that kind of neighborly attitude while they'd toured Europe's big cities. While the villagers and townsmen of third-world countries reminded him of the inhabitants of Chance Creek in the way they helped each other, the city folk were more aloof.

Inside, he check on Sunshine and found her asleep, so he joined the Cruzes for dinner and helped clean up. Then he said good-night to Autumn and gave Arianna, a bright-eyed little girl who took after her mother, a peck on the cheek, and headed upstairs.

Sunshine was still tucked into bed when he came in. All the lights were off except a soft glow emanating from an ornate lamp on the bedside table. It looked like she'd eaten the light meal Autumn had carried up to her. Her hair was a slash of gold across the plum-colored duvet cover as she slept.

Cole got ready quietly and took a quick shower. He dried off and climbed in beside her, trying hard not to wake her, but Sunshine stirred.

"Good-night," she whispered and turned over. Her breathing evened out just moments later.

Cole kissed her softly. "Good-night."

"YOU DON'T HAVE to help," Autumn said the next morning as Sunshine emptied the dishwasher in the large professional kitchen downstairs.

"It's my pleasure. You're so busy—whoops!" She just caught herself from dropping a stack of clean plates. "Oh my gosh, I'm sorry, Arianna!" She had nearly tripped over the little girl.

Arianna grinned up at her. Dressed in a light blue jumper and striped stockings, she was adorable. Her tiny pig tails stuck up from her head like mushrooms and her blue eyes shone with mischief.

"Come up here, pumpkin." Autumn lifted her up and put her in a high chair stationed next to the counter. "I hate to corral her," she confessed to Sunshine, "but she has the uncanniest ability to be right where my feet are at all times." She gave Arianna a coloring book and a pack of crayons. "That'll keep her occupied for about thirty seconds."

"How on earth do you get everything done?"

Sunshine watched Autumn move a mile a minute, chopping vegetables in preparation for the salad she was making for lunch. She picked up her own pace and finished emptying the dishwasher. She loved the way Autumn had decorated the large guest house for the holidays. There were boughs of greenery on the mantel and stair railing, threaded with red and silver beaded chains. The tree was massive, hung with rustic ornaments. Touches of red, green and gold shimmered everywhere she looked. Sunshine could picture the great room as a spread in a holiday decorating magazine.

"I have help most days." Autumn looked over her shoulder. "If you could clear the table and load the dishwasher, that would be great."

Sunshine matched her pace to Autumn's, but she was only half-finished when Arianna chucked the box of crayons across the room.

"Uh oh!" the little girl crowed, and threw the coloring book after them.

"Uh oh, my foot." But Autumn kissed her daughter's head. "Now what do you want to do, honey?"

"Down! Down!"

With a sigh, Autumn complied and set Arianna on her feet. "Go pick up those crayons."

"No!"

"That's her favorite word," she told Sunshine. "Watch your step."

"I will." Sunshine deposited her load of dishes in the dishwasher, then gathered the crayons.

"Thanks." Autumn had finished making the salad and was cracking eggs into a bowl. "So Ethan says you used to run a vegan restaurant. Will you reopen it?"

"It was more like a café. In the front of the rifle range, if you can believe it."

"Ethan's told me all about it. He said you and Cole had a rocky beginning, but then you fell in love." She whipped the eggs into a smooth froth.

"That's pretty much how it went. Then, after we'd lived together for a few months, we discovered my aunt had left us another inheritance. We took the cash and traveled the world. I wanted to see how people in indigenous cultures cooked. I had this idea that getting back to basics would teach me about the essence of food, and maybe life, too."

"Did it work?"

"For a little while." Sunshine moved back to the table and picked up another stack of dishes. "Then I got scared."

"What happened?" Autumn crossed to the stove and turned it on. "I'm assuming you don't want part of this omelette. Is there anything else I can get you? I never get to eat at breakfast time when I'm feeding everyone else." She put a pan on a burner and gave it a moment to heat before adding a pat of butter to it.

"I'm full, thanks. Breakfast was wonderful." Autumn was a thoughtful cook and she'd served several vegan offerings. Sunshine had discovered she was starving and devoured them. She'd enjoyed chatting with the other guests, too. Autumn's business was obviously doing well. Sunshine placed the dishes into the machine. "Anyway, I think it was the simplicity of it all. The people were living in primitive conditions that would render me suicidal if I knew I was stuck there, and not only were they surviving— they were laughing. And singing. And raising children. I don't want to romanticize it, because poverty isn't romantic at all. But..." She searched for words. "There's a difference between what you want and what you need." She rolled her eyes. "God, that's a song, isn't it? I guess everything was so raw it really became clear. Too clear."

"What became clear?"

"How spoiled rotten I am. How trivial I am. I want beautiful things. I want a beautiful home. I want to be up to date on the latest fashions and hop from trend to trend. I want a shiny stainless-steel kitchen in a restaurant so avant-guard that just being in it shocks your senses. And here were all these people cooking over fires and focusing on the things that really matter."

"Wow. That's some pretty heavy stuff." Autumn concentrated on her omelette, but

Sunshine knew she was listening to every word. "Still, Cole says you spent over a year in those kind of places before heading for Europe."

"You should have seen Cole. He fit right in everywhere we went. He could talk about herding animals and living off the land and hunting and protecting the ones you love. Everywhere he went he talked guns with the men."

Autumn chuckled. "I can imagine."

"The thing is, he could live like that. Forever. A tent, a fire, a gun, a set of clothes. He'd be fine. He'd work all day, provide for his family, come home at night and sit out under the stars. He'd make a few friends and be content."

"But you wouldn't?" Autumn said softly.

"For a minute there I thought I could. It scared me to death. It was like I had no ambition at all. I wanted to just… be."

"Is that so bad?"

"It is for me. I don't want to be a housewife. Besides, there's one big difference between them and us."

Autumn slid the omelette onto a plate. "What's that?"

"They're never alone. There's always another set of hands. A grandmother to hold the baby while you cook. A niece to run for water or wood. A friend to chat with on your way to the market. Again, I don't want to romanticize it. It wasn't romantic at all. Those women work so hard."

"But they have company."

"Right." Sunshine was lost in thought for a moment. "I can't help thinking that when I start a family, it'll all be on me. I'll have to run my restaurant—if I have one—take care of my child, do the housework—how will I handle it all?"

"Cole will be there." Autumn bit into her omelette. "Yum. That's good if I do say so myself."

"He'll have his own work," Sunshine protested.

"Here's the thing; you're right—it is hard to balance home and family and work. I'm lucky because I don't have to leave home to get my work done, and because I've been able to hire help. But I also have friends right here on the property. I guess my situation is a little like the one you're describing with those women. I watch Lynn or Jack, sometimes both. Claire and Morgan's children," she clarified when Sunshine looked at her blankly. "They watch Arianna in turn." She grew serious. "In this day and age you have to be imaginative to create a life that works. Finding ways to share the workload is definitely a start." She took another bite and chewed. "So, what happened in the end? Did you ever go back to the more rustic places?"

Sunshine frowned. "I spent the rest of the

trip dragging Cole around Europe—Munich and Paris and Rome and London," she confessed. "As far away from those little villages as I could get."

"You have to be true to yourself. Otherwise you'll be miserable. If you're a city girl, you're a city girl." Autumn waved her fork in emphasis.

She wasn't going to be one anymore, though. Not now that she'd bought the ranch. "You used to be a city girl, right?" Hadn't Autumn lived in New York before she met Ethan?

"Emphasis on *used to be*. When I met Ethan I was dying to have a baby, and this is exactly the kind of life I want to live now. I'm pregnant again, which means things will get even more hectic, but I know what I want—a big family. I'll forgo sleep—and Fifth Avenue—if that's what it takes."

Autumn was pregnant? Sunshine longed to share her own news, but she didn't think she should tell anyone before she'd told Cole. Instead, she said, "Can you keep a secret?"

"Of course."

"I bought Cole a ranch for Christmas."

"You did?" Autumn plunked her plate down on the counter. "Does that mean you're staying in Chance Creek?"

"Ye-" Sunshine shrieked when Autumn leapt across the kitchen to give her a bear hug. Arianna laughed and danced around them.

"I'm so glad! Ethan and the others were afraid they'd lose Cole all over again if you decided you liked Chicago better. They thought maybe you just came back to sell the shooting range and apartments."

"No." She took a deep breath, surprised at Autumn's excited reaction. She hadn't said this out loud yet. "I've decided we should stay. I mean, we decided." She made a face. "Actually, Cole has always been clear he wanted to live in Chance Creek. I was the one on the fence, but I've made up my mind and I plan to stick with it."

As she said the words, she hoped they were true.

"That's a big step. Are you sure you're okay with it?"

"Yes. My trip convinced me," Sunshine said staunchly. "Those city women in Europe should have been happier, but somehow it was the country women who were." She hoped she'd be happy too.

"It's all the fresh air," Autumn said. "Makes our husbands frisky." She returned to her omelette.

"Is that the secret?" Sunshine pretended to think it over. "Cole must have saved it up over the years. City, country—doesn't seem to make a difference."

Autumn laughed. "That's because he loves

you. So—are you going to get married?"

Sunshine turned back to her task. "We haven't set a date." She hoped to do so soon. In a perfect world it would all be settled before she told him about the baby, but since she'd always said they should wait to marry until after their trip, she couldn't blame Cole for holding off.

"Let me know as soon as you do."

"You can't tell anyone about the ranch. It's his Christmas present."

"I'll keep my mouth shut. But when do I get to see it?"

"Any time. I need to pick up the keys and get over there to check it out. The house needs a lot of work and there's so little time. I could use some help."

"I'd be glad to help!" When the front door opened, Autumn glanced at the clock. "That must be Claire here to get you. Are you all packed? Cole said he'd follow you over later. He wanted to help Ethan with the chores."

"Okay." She envied her fiancé's clear knowledge of who he was and what he liked. Would she ever know herself so well? "I'll run up and get our bags."

"How about I come get you after lunch and we can go look at the place together?" Autumn trailed her to the stairs.

"That sounds wonderful. Thanks." Once again, a vision of Fran came uninvited into her mind. Had she jumped the gun buying a house and property?

She forced the thought away. She couldn't change what she'd done now.

A half hour later, her luggage deposited in a spare bedroom, Sunshine followed Claire, a slender woman with sleek, dark hair that fell to her shoulders, on a tour through her home. Sunshine thought Claire was as fashionable as her house, with an air of contentment that suited her.

"We built the house a couple of years ago, when Jamie bought into the ranch," Claire said as they walked through the first floor.

"All of Cole's friends seem to have grown up so much while I've been gone. Not that they were childish," Sunshine rushed to add.

Claire laughed. "Ethan and his friends seemed like children to me back then—until suddenly they weren't. I guess while they grew up, I got younger. At least, I feel younger these days than I used to."

Sunshine secretly agreed. Wedding photos of Claire and Jamie hung in the living room. In them Claire looked far more severe. Back then her hair had been cut in a blunt bob and she'd been thin enough her cheekbones stood out. She was softer now.

"Jamie must be doing something right." Sunshine spun in a slow circle, taking in the living room. "This is beautiful. It's obvious you're an interior designer. How on earth do you keep things so clean when you have a toddler? And what have you done with your daughter?" The log house was decorated in a distinctly western style with authentic weavings on the walls and a color palette of burnt reds, sienna browns and mustard yellows. A tree in one corner of the room was decorated with western themed ornaments. Tiny hand-crafted saddles, boots, and horses hung from its boughs.

"It's never this clean normally," Claire confessed with a laugh. "I hired a service to come in and help for once because we've got company coming. Between my work and caring for Lynn, the house is usually a disaster. Lynn's in daycare today because I wanted to show you something. We'll pick her up on our way home."

"Our way home from where?"

"You'll see."

Chapter Three

"SO ETHAN TELLS me your horse breeding business is going gangbusters," Cole said to Jamie when they met up in the stables on the Cruz ranch. "You got a horse to sell me?"

"You got a place to put it?" Jamie cocked back his hat. He had a wiry build and dark hair, and the countenance of a man who spent his days outdoors. "Business is going well. But I've been working with horses in these parts since I could stand up. People know exactly who they're dealing with when they buy from me."

Cole was glad Jamie didn't seem to expect an answer to his question about a place to put a horse. He wasn't ready to talk about buying a ranch until he knew if he could afford one.

"From what I hear, this isn't the time to try to get into raising cattle."

Jamie led the way down the row to a stall where an Appaloosa stuck his head over the door curiously. "This is Achilles."

"Something wrong with his heel?"

"Nope." Jamie grinned. "He's strong. Great work horse. As for cattle…" He shook his head. "I wouldn't recommend it."

"Would you recommend horse breeding?"

Jamie shook his head again. "And not because I'm afraid of the competition. It's just there's already too many men in the game. I'll be all right because I'm established, but three other outfits opened up just this past year. That's too many."

"Hell, maybe I should just be a farmer instead."

He expected Jamie to protest. Instead, Jamie turned thoughtful. "Since we've got company coming tomorrow, I called around to find you another place to go. Rob's got a room. You should talk to him; he and Morgan have started a vineyard, you know. They're a few years off from making wine, but they're putting it all together."

"A vineyard." Cole was impressed. "I guess I will talk to him."

"How about a ride?"

"Hell, yeah. It's been far too long."

Cole helped Jamie to saddle up and soon they were picking their way down a snowy trail. It felt damn good to have a horse beneath him. Cole could make sense of the world perched up here.

"You should see my daughter ride," Jamie called back over his shoulder.

"Your daughter? She can't be old enough for that!"

"Nineteen months. I ride with her, but she's not scared at all. She loves it. I swear she talks to the horses and they talk back to her."

"Jamie Lassiter, a family man. Who would have thought it?"

"I love it. I want more, but Claire says we have to space them out."

Cole directed his horse to follow Jamie's lead. Once again he felt a twinge of jealousy. Would his ranch—should he manage to buy one—ever ring with children's voices?

He sure hoped so.

"What do you think? About the horse?" Jamie asked.

"I'll take him. Just as soon as I have a home to bring him to."

"WHAT IS IT?" Sunshine asked, looking around the small, empty building Claire had brought her to. It fronted on Main Street, but whatever purpose it once had, it had been stripped clean. She'd called Autumn to tell her she'd be out with Claire for a while. They were still slated to meet and take a look at the ranch later.

"A restaurant!" Claire spun around. "Look at the place. It's perfect! Central location. Great layout. I thought you'd be able to see the possibilities. Granted, there was another space that was much better, but it got snapped up a week or so ago, unfortunately. Still, I think this one has a lot of potential."

"I thought you were an interior designer, not a realtor."

"I am, but I've got friends in the business, and one of them mentioned it the other day. When I heard you were coming, I knew you had to see it. It's a very reasonable price." She named a figure.

Claire was right; compared to a restaurant in Chicago, it was very reasonable, but after putting a hefty deposit on a ranch, she couldn't afford a place like this. "The renovations would be expensive."

Claire rattled off another number. "I priced out appliances and tables and chairs. Everything. Top of the line, of course."

"Of course." Sunshine shook her head. "I'm sorry, Claire. It was really thoughtful of you to go through all the trouble, but I don't have that kind of money."

"Really? I thought you had a sizable inheritance."

"I did, but I spent it." Despite herself, she walked around the space, running her hand over the counter where the hostess station would be, and doing a quick mental calculation of the number of patrons she could seat. In truth, the restaurant was kind of small. She'd always hoped to run a larger establishment, but this was Chance Creek, after all. Maybe this was as big as she could get.

"On your trip?"

"No—on a ranch." She explained what she'd done. "It's Cole's Christmas present. I hope he likes it."

"Your trip must have changed you." Claire followed her around the room. "From what I heard I never thought you'd settle down in Chance Creek. I expected you to run away again the first chance you got."

"But you showed me a restaurant?"

"You need something to keep you here."

That seemed to be the general consensus, Sunshine thought. "I was a city girl," she said slowly. "Maybe I'll always be, but you learn things about yourself when you travel."

"Well, too bad you can't buy this place. I think it's got real possibilities."

Claire was right. She could make something special out of it, but first things first—they needed a home. Someday she'd get a real restaurant.

Maybe.

After watching how hard Autumn had to work to balance her job with raising her daughter—and the way Claire had to pay for childcare to get her job done—she wasn't sure about anything anymore. Maybe she'd have to shelve her dreams until the baby grew up.

"Thanks for showing it to me," was all she said to Claire.

"I'd love to see the ranch you bought."

"I'd love to get your professional opinion about the house," Sunshine said. "If you don't mind, we could go pick up the keys right now. Then we can meet up with Autumn and go see it."

Claire agreed and an hour later all three women, and Arianna, were on their way to the ranch. Away from the restaurant, and too busy chatting with the others to think about Fran, excitement buoyed her mood and she clasped her gloved hands together to keep from fidgeting. This wasn't just going to be Cole's ranch, after all. This was going to be her home—her family's home. She wanted to love it and she was anxious she might have chosen badly.

Autumn, sitting behind her in the back of Claire's car, leaned forward and squeezed her shoulder. "It'll be great," she said.

"I hope so. Maybe I was stupid to buy it before I even walked the property." Her realtor had told her to make an offer fast, though, if she wanted it. Ranches didn't last long in this market and someone else had expressed an interest.

Arianna, in her car seat, squealed happily as they pulled up in front of the place. Sunshine wished she could, too. They had to park on the street because the lane hadn't been plowed. The house was set back from the street, but just like in the photographs online it sat proud and square on the property. Their boots crunched as they walked up the long driveway and an icy breeze made her shiver. It definitely felt like Christmas.

"Oh, I love it," Autumn said.

"It's not fancy, like your house. Or anywhere near as grand as yours, Claire," Sunshine said, but she too immediately felt the charm of it. The main house was two stories, its clapboard siding painted white and the trim around the windows and door a forest green. The door itself was black with a plain wreath on it. Sunshine wondered if a realtor had put it up in deference to the season. On one side, a single-story wing jutted out from the house. Sunshine knew from the photographs she'd seen it contained a family room that had been added on to the structure. The builders had done a good job integrating it into the rest of the house, however. The siding, paint and trim all matched perfectly.

The front porch was generous. Sunshine imagined flowers massed in front of it and shrubs to either side of the steps. She'd put up hanging baskets every spring—and maybe a birdhouse, too.

"Let's go. I can't wait to see inside," Autumn said, breaking into her thoughts.

Sunshine was so nervous when they got to

the front door, she fumbled with the keys before she could open it. Finally she unlocked it and stepped over the threshold.

"Oh, it's lovely," Claire said, coming in behind her.

Sunshine was so thankful to hear her say so. She loved it, too. The entryway was flanked by a living room to the right and a dining room to the left.

"A perfect Colonial," Autumn said. "It's similar to Crescent Hall. Have you met the Halls, Sunshine?"

"Minus a floor and about half the square footage," Claire said. She bit her lip. "I mean, not that this is small."

"It's okay," Sunshine assured her. "I haven't met the Halls, but I'm not jealous of their big house. This is perfect for us, because we don't have a big family. Besides, it has four bedrooms and two bathrooms. Plenty of room for us to grow into."

"That sounds wonderful." Autumn led the way into the dining room. "I love the wainscoting and the chair rail."

"I'm not such a fan of the color," Claire said critically.

"Which is why I brought you," Sunshine said. "Let's brainstorm as we go. I want cheerful colors, but not wild ones." They passed into the kitchen and all three stopped short.

"Well, it'll need a little updating," Autumn said tentatively.

"You mean it needs to be gutted. Sunshine, I hope you got a discount on the place," Claire said in dismay.

Sunshine swallowed in a suddenly dry throat. She had gotten the place for a reasonable price, but *reasonable* when you were talking about a ranch wasn't that cheap. The pictures had made it clear she'd need new appliances, and so had her realtor, but Sunshine hadn't realized the kitchen would be this bad. The countertop was badly scarred, several shelves were missing from the cabinets and the linoleum floor was turning yellow with age.

"Well, so much for having the place done by Christmas," she said.

"Not completely done but you can spiff it up a lot," Autumn said.

"Autumn's right. Some new paint and a whole lot of cleaning will go a long way. You and Cole can pick out appliances together," Claire said.

"We'll all help you get as far as you can." Autumn shifted Arianna to her other hip. The little girl surveyed the place with interest, wriggling as if she'd like to get down. "Claire, you can help pick out colors and arrange for the painting to be done. Sunshine will oversee the project, of course, but we'll all stop by whenever we can and help clean it up before the contractors come."

Autumn's words were music to Sunshine's ears. "Do you really think that would work?"

"We need to make an overall plan. We'll clean and paint before Christmas, then do the rest afterward," Claire said thoughtfully. "I'll squeeze your project in."

"But you can't tell the men," Sunshine rushed to say. "Cole absolutely can't know a thing about it until Christmas morning."

"No one will spill the beans," Autumn said.

They moved on to tour the rest of the ground floor. Sunshine loved the formal living room, but the family room was so cozy with its huge fireplace she knew they'd end up spending most of their time there. Upstairs they found the bedrooms generous, although the closets were small.

"You'll need to buy a wardrobe or two," Claire noted. "I'll be sure to send you links to some examples."

"That's a great idea." Sunshine was thankful Claire was being so positive.

They returned to the front hall. "Thank you both so much," Sunshine told them.

"No problem. It's exciting. I wish I could be there when Cole sees his present," Autumn said.

"Where are you spending Christmas?" Claire asked.

"I don't know. We'd booked our hotel room

through the holidays, but now that's not an option."

"Well, that's simple," Autumn told her. "You'll stay with us. One of our rooms opens up Christmas Eve."

"Thank you." Sunshine was overwhelmed by her generosity.

"Don't mention it—"

All three women turned around when a loud knock sounded on the front door.

"Who could that be?" Sunshine stepped to the front entrance, afraid Cole had somehow tracked her down. When she opened the door, a man she didn't recognize stood outside.

"Carl? What are you doing here?" Autumn asked.

"Are you Sunshine Patterson?" Carl asked, ignoring Autumn. He was a tall, rugged-looking man and Sunshine estimated he was in his thirties. He had a sharp, no-nonsense air.

"Yes."

"Glad to finally meet you."

"What's going on?" Claire asked. "Is something wrong, Carl?"

Sunshine knew why she asked; the man looked displeased. "I'm here to make Sunshine an offer. I'll pay double what you did for this ranch. In cash. Today."

Sunshine's mouth dropped open. "Why?"

"Because I want it. I was supposed to buy

it—I don't know how you got the jump on me."

"I told my realtor I wanted to make an offer. When I did, it was accepted." There wasn't anything underhanded about it, but Carl's tone suggested he thought there was.

"Well, now I've offered you twice as much to sell it to me."

"You can't just barge in here and try to take Sunshine's ranch," Claire said. "This isn't California, Carl."

"Money talks all over, Claire. And I want this ranch. I've been trying to buy land around here since I let go of my old place. I keep losing out."

He was obviously distressed about the situation and Sunshine felt bad for the man, but that didn't mean she would sell to him…

Or should she?

Once again she thought of the bright, modern restaurant she could buy in Chicago. The hordes of patrons she could feed. The write-ups she might get in the city papers—or even the national ones.

Did she really want to trade all that for a ranch—in Chance Creek where women like Fran held sway?

"Double the money," Carl said again. "If you sign it over today."

"Carl, that's crazy," Claire said.

"I'm afraid I can't do that," Sunshine said, although the thought of turning down all that money made her a little dizzy. She consoled herself that the man had to be joking. No one would pay double for her little ranch.

"Of course you can't; this is your new home," Autumn said.

"Are you sure?" A muscle worked in Carl's jaw. "Don't you want to even think about it? I'm good for the cash; either of these women can vouch for me."

Autumn and Claire, both looking unhappy, nodded. "It's true; Carl can afford it," Claire said. "But he should wait and find a ranch of his own."

"I think you should take some time to think it over," Carl said to Sunshine. "What do you say?"

She couldn't help but nod. "Okay—I'll think about it. Just for a day or two."

Carl pulled out his wallet and handed her a card, the look of satisfaction on his face telling her he thought he'd won. "Take your time—within reason, of course."

"She doesn't want to sell the ranch," Autumn told him.

"She might," Claire said slowly. "Sunshine wants a restaurant."

"I'll help find you one," Carl told her. "Call me, day or night." He left as suddenly as he'd arrived.

Autumn shut the door behind him. "He's

had a bad string of luck with property," she explained. "Ethan told me he's lost out on a couple of places, and Carl's not accustomed to losing when it comes to money."

"That's a hell of a deal he offered you," Claire said. "You might want to take it. There'll be other ranches, sooner or later."

"Don't do it," Autumn said. "They don't come up that often and most of them are a lot bigger, and a lot more expensive. This place isn't big enough for Carl, anyway; he's just getting desperate. He'd sell it again the minute he found another one."

"I don't remember seeing him before." Sunshine walked back into the kitchen to survey it again. After Carl's offer it looked even more woebegone. Was she crazy not to take him up on the deal? Maybe the place wasn't right for them after all.

"He arrived in town right after you and Cole left. Stole Ethan's fiancée away from him, thank goodness," Autumn said. "Then he lost her."

"That's the man who stole Lacey? Wow." She wondered why Lacey had left him. From everything she'd heard about the woman, Lacey liked the finer things in life.

"Should we start making lists of things to do?" Autumn asked her.

Claire checked the time. "I have to go pick up Lynn."

"And I should probably think about it over-night," Sunshine added.

"Don't do anything rash," Autumn said.

Too late, Sunshine thought.

"DID YOU HAVE a good time with Claire?" Cole asked late that night when they were heading to bed. Sunshine had been quiet all evening, which worried him. Down the hall, baby Lynn was crying. A small, dark-haired sprite, she'd been tearful on and off since late in the afternoon, which had made everyone a little tense. He was ready for bed, but first he wanted to make sure Sunshine was all right. He'd come home to find her and Claire sitting at the kitchen table having a heated discussion. There was a piece of paper between them with two columns on it. He'd only gotten the chance to read the headings—*pros* and *cons*—before Sunshine snatched it off the table and crumpled it up. When he'd tried to find out what they were up to, they'd refused to answer his questions. The whole incident left him uneasy.

"I did." She turned down the covers of the bed, rummaged through her suitcase and gathered her toiletries. Lynn's wails hit a high note, subsided for a moment, and started again. "Poor little girl. She sounds over-tired."

"She sure does." Cole stood a moment in front of one of the tall windows. It was dark outside, but the contours of the land were visible in the starlight. "Can't beat the view from here." Pasture spread out as far as the eye could see. In the distance were mountains—dark shapes against an inky sky. "Nothing says home like this."

Sunshine sighed and Cole frowned. Didn't she feel the same way? Something had been off about her for the last couple of weeks. Cole didn't know what it was, but after his conversation with Ethan yesterday he was beginning to worry she didn't want to settle in Chance Creek after all. Suddenly he needed to know. Instinct told him this wasn't the time—not with Lynn's wails building up into a crescendo—but he couldn't help himself.

"This is home, isn't it?" he asked, watching Sunshine carefully for her reaction to the question.

She just shrugged and kept looking through her suitcase.

"I had assumed we were in agreement about that." He crossed his arms over his chest and leaned against the window frame.

Sunshine stood up. "You know what they say about assumptions." Her tone was teasing, but Cole's frown deepened. What did that mean? Was she saying she didn't want to live here?

As Lynn's cries turned into high pitched screams, Sunshine headed toward the bathroom.

Were Claire and Jamie torturing that baby? Probably just changing a diaper or something, he decided. He felt bad for them; they had more company coming in the morning and they needed a good night's sleep.

"Are you saying you want to live in Chicago?" God, he hoped not. He'd do a lot for Sunshine, but he didn't think he could endure that.

"I'm saying let's take a little time to decide where we want to live." She paused at the bathroom and glanced toward the door to the hall, frowning as Lynn's wails went on and on. Cole knew how she felt. He wanted to stride down to the nursery room, take the baby and fix the problem, whatever it was.

"I thought you were ready to settle down." Damn, that was gruffer than he'd meant to be, but the baby's cries were really getting to him.

Sunshine looked almost guilty as she turned toward the bathroom again. "It's almost Christmas, Cole. Let's wait to figure things out until after the holidays."

He wasn't sure how to interpret that. Maybe he should give up the topic for tonight and try again tomorrow. He was tired. So was Sunshine. And the queen-sized bed looked all too inviting. Should he simply lead Sunshine over to it, undress her and celebrate their love the way they had so many times before?

Judging from her body language—and the screams down the hall—the answer was no. There wouldn't be any lovemaking tonight.

"Something's been bugging me," he heard himself say. It was as if the baby's screams were chiseling away at his common sense. This was no time for a serious conversation, but now he'd started, he didn't know how to stop. "I saw the way you handled small village life. You were a trooper, and for a while I thought you fit in there pretty well. Then everything changed. Why was that?" It was something they should have discussed long before, but when Sunshine first dragged him to a city after their wilderness adventures, he'd been so busy enjoying hot showers and European cuisine, he hadn't thought to ask. He'd thought it was going to be a brief change before they plunged into the grittier aspects of travel again, but it hadn't been.

Sunshine shrugged. "I can deal with any hardship for a little while. Then it gets too much."

Lynn let out a series of screams like a haywire teakettle. Cole lost his cool.

"Is that how you see Chance Creek? Like a hardship? Jesus, what is wrong with that kid?"

"Of course not." She made a face. "Cole, she's a baby. She's overtired. Sometimes they have to scream it out."

"Thank God we don't have children."

She recoiled and Cole stifled a curse. That wasn't what he'd meant to say at all. He wanted kids. Someday. When they were ready for them. "I mean tonight. I don't think I could handle that tonight."

"With a baby you don't get a choice about when you want to handle it." She disappeared into the bathroom. Cole followed her and stopped her from shutting the door.

"Let's get back to the real topic. I thought we were going to make a life here together."

"I thought so, too."

What the hell did that mean? Cole had lost all sense of the conversation and the baby's screams weren't helping. They'd had such a good time in this town together before they left on their trip. They'd been head over heels in love—

Cole's thoughts skidded to a halt. Was that the problem? Had Sunshine fallen out of love with him? She'd been plotting something with Claire this afternoon. He'd thought it had to do with Christmas. Was he wrong?

"Look, Cole. I'd like to be by myself." She indicated the bathroom door. "Do you mind?"

He retreated, the floor suddenly unsteady beneath his feet. Sunshine shut the door firmly— then locked it with a loud click.

Well, that sent a clear message. She didn't want him around. Maybe she was sick of him.

As Lynn shrieked in a series of ear-splitting

wails, Cole crossed the room in three steps, pulled open the door and left. If Sunshine wanted space, he'd give her space.

A whole lot of it.

THANK GOD WE *don't have kids.*

Cole's words boomeranged around Sunshine's brain as she paced the bathroom floor, trying to shut out Lynn's wailing down the hall. Her brain told her Cole didn't mean it. He was tired and angry, and Lynn's screams would drive a saint to blasphemy. But her heart was as sore as if he'd stomped on it. She tried to remind herself of how good he'd been with the children they'd met on their travels. Like the night he'd played soccer barefoot with a straggling group of children in a tiny village on the edge of the Sahara Desert, or the way he'd created a bat out of a stick of wood and taught the children of a Nepalese settlement American baseball.

Cole shone with kids as long as the setting was bucolic, she realized. He'd avoided them like the plague once they'd hit the city centers of Europe.

Why?

The answer came all too easily, summed up in a statement he'd made one day in London as they passed a playground surrounded by chain link fence.

"Is that a school or a prison?" he'd asked.

"You know it's a school," she'd said, annoyed by the question.

"But do those kids?"

She wanted to rail against his words the way Lynn was protesting her bedtime, although Lynn seemed to be finally winding down, her cries lacking the volume they'd achieved previously. Cities weren't so bad; Sunshine had grown up in one and she'd loved it. Pastures and horses weren't required for a childhood.

Although they were nice.

As Lynn's crying finally subsided, Sunshine admitted something she'd refused to think about since she'd taken the pregnancy test.

By choosing Cole—and parenthood—was she saying no to the career she'd always thought she had? Cole had made it all too clear he didn't want to put his children into daycare, but where did that leave her? She'd always seen herself as a career woman. She'd gone on their round-the-world trip to become a better chef. Just because she was pregnant, did she have to give that up?

They'd never actually hashed out how they'd handle children, and if she was honest, that was one reason she been in no hurry to tell him about her pregnancy. Of course it was going to be fun to reveal it along with the ranch she'd bought on Christmas morning, but by waiting she'd also been able to put off the day they'd have to discuss the arrangements for after the baby was born.

She'd tried to believe she could be happy regardless of where they lived, or whether or not she worked. But if Cole didn't even want children, all bets were off. She might as well take Carl's money and run.

That triggered a whole new line of thinking. Should she accept Carl's offer? Cole would never have to know she'd even bought the ranch in the first place. She could turn around, demand they move to Chicago and have the restaurant she'd always wanted. Why should she be the one to put off all her dreams?

When she exited the bathroom, she hadn't decided anything, and Cole still hadn't returned. She turned out the lights and climbed into bed, prepared to wait and question him. She wouldn't tell him about her pregnancy, but she could find out where he stood on children—and on marriage in general.

She'd always thought that Cole was a man who could handle commitment, but Fran's stories had shaken her to the core. Back in high school, at least, he'd been nothing but a good-time boy. When she'd met him he'd still been a confirmed bachelor.

Why did she think he'd change for her?

She woke up to find the night had passed and light was streaming in through the windows. It was eight in the morning and Sunshine sat up, still half-asleep but fully aware that something was wrong.

"Cole?" she whispered, unsure if the others were awake yet. She turned to his side of the bed...

And found it empty.

Not only empty, but unslept in. While her covers were mussed, his side of the bed remained untouched. Sunshine's heart sank. They hadn't slept apart since the day they became engaged. Where had Cole gone?

Was he coming back?

She slipped out of the bed and dressed hurriedly, twisting her hair into a quick braid to hide the fact she hadn't showered. Stepping to the window and lifting the shade, she scanned as much of the ranch as she could from this vantage point.

No sign of him.

Her heart heavy, she opened her door and slipped out into the hall. When she came downstairs she nearly gasped in relief when she saw him seated at the breakfast table. There was a plate in front of him and a half-drunk glass of orange juice. French toast sat on a serving tray, but neither Claire nor Jamie was around.

"Good morning," she said, feeling as if she was greeting a stranger.

"Morning." Cole set down the newspaper he was reading.

She wanted to ask him where he'd spent the night but she was afraid of the answer. To cover her confusion she served herself a glass of juice. The French toast obviously wasn't vegan and she didn't feel like eating, even if she knew she should eat something to keep up her strength.

She sat down at the table across from him, not knowing what else to do.

"I've got errands to do this morning. Think you can handle the move to Rob and Morgan's place?" he said.

"Sure." Did he want her to ask about his errands? Because she wasn't going to. Not when he was speaking to her so gruffly—as if she'd done something wrong.

"Okay." He drained his cup and stood up. "See you later."

He left without even dropping a kiss on top of her head. Had he ever done that before? Sunshine was too stunned to answer her own question. When Claire walked in a few minutes later, Lynn in her arms, Sunshine was still sitting motionless at the table.

"Don't you want some breakfast?" Claire asked as she popped Lynn into her high chair. "I've got fruit and cereal if the French toast is too heavy."

"I'm fine, thanks." Fine was the last thing she was. "Is Lynn feeling better today?"

"Much. I hope she didn't keep you up too

late." Claire fetched a box of cereal and put a handful of O's on the tray in front of Lynn. Lynn began to pick them up one by one and eat them, watching Sunshine with big, round eyes.

"I got plenty of sleep." Her pregnancy was as good as a sleeping aid these last few days.

"I think she's cutting a tooth. Maybe a molar." Claire moved around the kitchen, piling up dirty dishes in the sink.

Sunshine smiled tentatively at Lynn, although her stomach was in knots after her exchange with Cole. Or maybe that was morning sickness.

"Do you think it would be hard to be a single mom?" she asked, and wanted to smack herself the moment the question leaped from her lips.

Claire's eyebrows shot skyward. "I should guess so. Why?"

"Just thinking about a friend," Sunshine stuttered. "At least you had Jamie to help you out last night."

Claire nodded. "I couldn't imagine doing it alone. Give me ten minutes to feed Lynn and I'll run you over to Morgan's, okay?"

Grateful for the excuse to do something, Sunshine stood up. "Thanks. I'll go pack."

"You'll like Morgan. You'll see."

"I'm sure I will."

Liking her next set of hosts was the least of her worries.

"I HOPE YOUR fiancée loves it," Terry said as he handed a ring of keys to Cole and stood back while Cole unlocked the front door. Escrow had finally closed and now he was the proud owner of a restaurant space. The realtor had come along to walk through it with him. He had some recommendations for contractors who could help Cole out with any renovations he might need. Cole entered the establishment, a large corner building on Main Street with its own parking lot, and fumbled for a light switch. As light flooded the place, Cole nodded. It looked much like the photographs he'd seen online before he bought it, but he wrinkled his nose.

"What's that smell?"

"I don't know. It didn't smell like this last time." The two men began to investigate. Up front was a hostess station and a number of battered tables and booths. The smell got stronger as they headed toward the rear of the restaurant.

"I don't like this," Terry said. "I think the sewer has backed up into one of the bathrooms."

He was right, and the results were dismal.

Cole covered his nose and mouth with his arm. "Hell, who do we call to fix this?"

"Already on it." They headed into the kitchen while Terry fished out his cell phone and tapped in a number. "Reggie? Got an emergency for you."

As Terry filled in the contractor, Cole looked around the kitchen. Everything was in good shape, but he'd need to test the appliances. The place even came with some dishes, utensils, pots and pans, but Cole suspected Sunshine would want to upgrade those.

If she ever cooked here.

He still couldn't figure out how their argument had gone from zero to a hundred so fast the previous night. He had gone over it again and again in his mind as he fought for sleep on Claire and Jamie's couch. He'd decided it had been his comment about kids that sent them into a tailspin. He'd better make his real position clear.

Kids.

Would they have kids? He'd been surprised by how much he'd enjoyed the children they'd met on their trip—especially the ones in the most remote areas. Free from the influence of television shows and the Internet, they wore their feelings and reactions right at the surface and he'd relaxed around so much honesty. They were active—and fun-loving. Cole felt that the teens he saw in Chance Creek were more self-conscious. That bothered him. If he had kids he'd want to emphasize honesty and plain speaking—and the fun that comes from playing outside and moving your body, rather than sitting like zombies in front of video games.

Still, kids were a big step and they weren't

even married yet. They had to set a date for the wedding.

Maybe he should take the lead on that.

"Okay, Reggie's sending a team as soon as he can. I'll drive by and drop off a set of keys with him. Go on home and relax. Let us take care of this. When it's all fixed and fresh as a daisy in here, I'll give you a call and we'll start again."

"I was hoping to fix a few things up before Christmas," Cole told him.

"We'll have you back in here tomorrow."

"Sounds good."

Cole drove to Rob and Morgan's house, a good-sized home they'd built on a plot of land on the Double-Bar-K, Rob's family's ranch. Cole found Rob on the front porch waiting for him, his hands jammed into the pockets of a heavy coat. Tall and muscular, with the blond hair typical of the Matheson men, Rob looked far more relaxed and confident than he had been when Cole last saw him three years ago.

"I was wondering where you'd got to," Rob said, shaking his hand. "It's good to see you, man. How'd you like traveling the world?"

"I feel mighty lucky to have had the chance, but now I'm happy to be home. I heard all about your vineyard and plans for a winery from Jamie. I'm impressed. I'd like to see the vines."

"Not a whole lot to see at this time of year, but I'd be glad to take you out for a look around." Rob opened the front door and they moved inside. "But you'll need Morgan to get the full picture. She's the mastermind behind this operation."

"Don't let Rob fool you. He's a wizard with the grapes," Morgan said, coming to greet Cole. "It's good to meet you. I've heard so much about you I feel like we're already friends."

"I hope we will be." Morgan had dark, wavy hair, blue eyes, and a way of moving that hinted at athleticism. Cole was pleased to see the way she and Rob smiled at each other when she came to lean against her husband, an arm around his waist. They were obviously in love. Cole was still surprised to find all his old friends settled down with wives when they used to be such bachelors.

Sunshine came to meet him, too, with a baby boy on her hip that had to be Jack. Cole's heart melted at the sweet picture they made, especially when she bent down to rub noses with the little boy and Jack squealed with laughter.

They really needed to have that talk about their future plans—including when to have kids. Sunshine would make a wonderful mother someday.

And he… he looked forward to being a father.

That idea startled him. Was he really ready? He hadn't thought so previously. To cover his confusion, he said, "Look at him. Big and strong like his daddy. You'll make a rancher out of that one."

"Damn straight," Rob said. "Jack loves horses."

"Jack loves everything," Morgan said. "We're so lucky. We've got the smilingest baby ever."

"He's darling," Sunshine said. "Aren't you?" She snuggled the little boy again, who grinned.

That smile hit Cole like a sucker punch. *I'm glad we don't have kids.* Had he really said that just last night? He was an ass. He wished they could get started on a family right away.

First, they needed to get married.

No, first he had to make up his fight with Sunshine, he realized. As soon as possible.

"Cole wants to see the vines," Rob told Morgan. "I've got some time. Let's head out to take a look."

Morgan bit her lip. "I have to change Jack and get him into his snowsuit."

"I'll keep him," Sunshine broke in. "You and Rob go on. I'll be fine."

Cole shot her a look. Why was she lagging back? Was she still tired? She seemed to be tired all the time these days. It was like she'd held it together for the entire trip, but now that they were home, Sunshine was collapsing under the strain. Maybe she needed a day or two in bed.

That sounded like a brilliant idea if he could get her to let him join her there.

"It'll take a while," Rob warned her. "It'll be slow going for us through the snow."

"Take as long as you want. We'll have fun, won't we, Jack?" Sunshine jiggled him on her hip and he crowed with laughter. Cole relaxed. Maybe she was fine, after all.

Maybe her biological clock was ticking, too.

Morgan showed Sunshine where to find diapers, wipes, food and juice, and imparted a hundred other bits of information, until Rob finally took her hand and tugged her playfully to the door. "We'll be back in an hour. I'm sure Sunshine can handle it."

"I'll be fine; don't worry about a thing."

When they finally made it outside, Rob fell back with Cole. "Mothers," he said in a low voice. "It's like they lose their minds when they have babies." His indulgent tone told Cole he adored Morgan's protective attitude. He seemed to love every minute of fatherhood.

Cole wanted to love it, too.

WHY, OH WHY hadn't she turned on the television before she walked Jack to sleep? Sunshine paced the length of the living room, turned around and paced it again. If she turned it on now she'd wake him up. Could she lay him down in his crib without waking him? She wasn't sure. Sunshine paced the room again.

Nearly two hours had passed since the others

left, and the quiet house was beginning to get to her. Even when they'd stopped in villages in Africa and Asia, there were always grandparents, aunts, uncles and cousins around. Only in a North American house did you get this kind of isolation. She was beginning to feel like she was the only person left in the world.

The only grownup, anyway.

She'd enjoyed playing with Jack. He certainly was an easy baby. Once he'd started to fuss she'd picked him up, changed him, fed him and then carried him around, delighting in the way he snuggled easily into her arms, trusting her to know what to do. She'd swayed and danced with him until he'd fallen asleep, a lovely experience, but now her arms ached from the unfamiliar exercise and she was growing tired. Aside from that, an idea for a new recipe had sprung into her head while she was pacing the floor with Jack and she itched to write it down before she forgot about it.

Sunshine tiptoed up the steps to the second floor where Jack's room was located next to the master bedroom. She eased him into his crib and was pleased and proud when he didn't wake up. Stepping carefully to the door, she swung it partway closed.

She made it halfway down the steps before Jack began to wail.

Sunshine stopped, torn between the desire to

race downstairs and jot down the recipe, and the need to placate Jack immediately. After all, Morgan had put her son's well-being into her care.

With a sigh, she retraced her steps, chanting the ingredients for the new dish in her mind, and scooped Jack back up from his crib. He laughed with glee and hugged her.

"You need a nap," she told him, but one look into his bright, cheerful eyes told her naptime was over. Jack was refreshed and ready to go again.

Too bad she wasn't.

Nausea had crept up on her, which frustrated Sunshine. Wasn't morning sickness supposed to happen in the early morning?

She'd also hoped to find a way out to the ranch to look around again today. She needed to make up her mind about whether to keep it or sell it to Carl. Claire and Autumn were standing by for a phone call. She needed to get Morgan alone to let her in on the secret, too.

She told herself the others would be home soon enough and she brought Jack back downstairs, gave him some toys and placed him on the living room rug. She ducked into the kitchen to find her purse, in which she had a pad of paper and a pen.

"Don't get into trouble," she called out to Jack as she jotted down the recipe in a kind of shorthand she hoped she'd be able to decipher later. She shoved the pad and pen back into her purse, and trotted back to the living room, ready to give Jack her undivided attention again, when her cell phone rang. Stopping, she fished it out. She didn't recognize the number, but she answered it—it could be Autumn or Claire.

"Sunshine? It's Carl Whitfield. Ready to make that deal yet?"

"I… haven't made up my mind." She hadn't had time to think about any of it properly.

"I'm really anxious to get that property."

"I know—" Sunshine looked around, suddenly aware something was wrong.

Where was Jack?

"Jack?" Sunshine scanned the room. "Jack!"

"Sunshine?"

She cut the call, shoved the phone in her pocket again and searched the room. Had he climbed the stairs? She realized she hadn't locked the baby gate after coming through it. With her heart in her mouth she raced up the steps two at a time. "Jack!" A quick look in each bedroom and bathroom told her he wasn't on the second floor. She raced back down again, did a circuit of the main floor, but didn't find him there either.

Panic clawed at her throat as she raced from room to room for a second time. Only then did she spot the glass sliding door off the den. It was ajar, and the curtains framing it fluttered as a light breeze slipped through it. "Jack!" Her scream came out like a squeak. The baby didn't have shoes on or a coat. And the ranch was covered in drifts of snow. She raced through the room and out the door, the slick surface of the deck immediately soaking through her socks. "Jack, where are you?"

A thin wail greeted her and Morgan raced down the steps to where Jack was standing in the snow, lifting first one soaked cold foot and then the other. She scooped him up, her heart beating double time. She didn't realize she was crying until Jack reached out to touch her cheeks. "Wet!"

"Yes, you're right. And so are your feet. And mine!" She hustled back up the steps, into the den, and came face to face with Morgan, Rob and Cole.

Chapter Four

"SUNSHINE—WHAT ARE YOU doing?" Cole was too shocked to censor his tone when Sunshine came through the sliding glass door in her stocking feet, a similarly shoeless Jack in her arms. When he, Rob and Morgan had arrived home, the house had been empty. Worry had lifted his heart into his throat.

"He… escaped," Sunshine said, clearly distraught.

Morgan rushed to take Jack from her arms.

"Weren't you watching him?" Cole said. He couldn't believe Sunshine had been so negligent. He'd just spent the last hour—two and a half hours, Cole realized with a jolt as he spotted a clock on the wall—learning everything Morgan and Rob could tell him about growing grapes and making wine. He'd had such a good time he'd forgotten about his problems with Sunshine until they'd approached the house again. Then they'd found the place empty—with Sunshine's coat and shoes clearly visible in the foyer. Cole had panicked.

"Of course I was—I just stepped into the other room for a minute!"

"You can't do that!" Cole couldn't seem to stop himself. He'd concocted an idea about going into business with Rob and Morgan, and he wanted them to like him—and to see him as a responsible individual. Sunshine was blowing it.

"I should have warned you he can open the sliding doors," Morgan said. "I told you we need to brace them shut," she said to Rob.

"I'll get on it today," Rob said. He turned to Sunshine. "Morgan told me Jack opened one last week. I guess I didn't quite believe it."

"I swear I was right with him almost the whole time. I stepped into the kitchen—"

"It's okay," Morgan assured her. "No harm done. Toddlers are a handful. Cole's right; you simply can't ever look away. Although, of course you have to now and then. You develop a kind of mommy sense when it's your child."

"I'm so sorry." Tears shone in Sunshine's eyes. Cole's heart contracted. Of course Sunshine had been doing a good job. He knew how responsible she was.

"It's our fault for leaving you alone so long," Rob said. He took Jack from Morgan's arms. "And I hope you learned your lesson, little man. When you run away you get cold, wet feet."

"Wet!" Jack crowed again, kicking up his heels.

Rob chuckled. "I'll go get him changed."

"I'll come with you," Cole said. He was too confused by his reaction to speak with Sunshine, and he wanted to apologize to Rob again for what had happened when they were alone. But when they reached the baby's room, Rob waved his words away.

"Believe me, this kid has gotten away from all of us a time or two. He's as slippery as a fish. Aren't you?"

Jack laughed and allowed Rob to change his pants and socks.

Cole decided to make the most of the opportunity. "I was thinking. Maybe there's a way I could work together with you and Morgan. I... think I'll get some land soon," he said. "We could plant some more vines on my land and you could teach me what I need to know to tend them."

Rob shook his head. "I appreciate the idea, but the vineyard is something that's going to take years to grow into a business that can support us, let alone someone else. I'm sorry, but we're stretched to the hilt and I promised Morgan we would keep things simple until we start to make a profit. I still help out Jamie and Ethan with their businesses, and Morgan helps Autumn. That's what keeps us solvent."

Cole nodded, trying to hide his disappointment. "I have to figure out something to do. If it's not cattle and it's not horses and it's not grapes, how can I earn a living? I don't want to go back to running the rifle range."

Rob thought about that. "Tell you what; you should talk to Evan Mortimer. The man's a genius and he's rich. He and Bella—you remember Bella Chatham right?—bought Carl Whitfield's old mansion when he decided to pack it in and return to California. Carl tried to get it back when he returned to town." Rob chuckled at the memory. "But Evan and Bella were too attached. Poor guy; he's been looking for a suitable place ever since. Anyway, they built a new veterinary hospital and shelter there, and Evan's working with Jake on sustainable ranching practices. He's got a herd of bison now that Jake helps him with and he's thinking of branching out to more specialty products. Between the two of them, they ought to have some ideas." He finished slipping socks over Jack's feet and stood the little boy up. "So, you and Sunshine are home for good, huh?"

"Definitely." He filled Rob in on the restaurant. "I've got my work cut out for me sprucing it up before Christmas. I'd better head to town in a few hours and make sure the contractor got that problem cleaned up."

"I'll come and give you a hand."

"HOW ON EARTH do you do it?" Sunshine asked when Morgan handed her a cup of tea. Her hands were still shaking and she thought she'd have nightmares tonight about losing Jack.

"Do what?"

"Work and be a mom? I can't believe you've started a winery and you don't have Jack in daycare."

"Rob and I work things out between us. I have a backpack Jack loves to ride around in, so I try to get as much done as possible with him in there. Then it's just a big balancing act. Sometimes I work early in the morning, sometimes late at night, sometimes while holding Jack and sometimes alone while Rob has him." She brought a second cup over to the table and sat down across from Sunshine.

"That sounds exhausting."

"It is. But I think it's worth it. I'm not ready to put Jack in daycare. That might change when he's a little older, though."

"Claire does it."

"Claire has to. There's no way she could tote a toddler around while she works in other people's houses."

"Can I ask you another question?" Sunshine fidgeted with her napkin.

"Sure." Morgan blew on her tea and took a sip.

"When you're at home with Jack alone, don't

you ever get lonely?"

"I did at first, but now I have a plan in place to prevent that. I call it Glepf." She set her cup back on the table.

"Could you spell that?" Sunshine laughed.

"G stands for girlfriends. When I realized I was starting to go stir-crazy, I went to every playgroup and mom activity there was and hit up all my other mother friends for their schedules until I had a list of at least ten moms I could call when I got bored, lonely or stressed out. L stands for lunch. It's hard to eat out with kids, but I can sometimes pull off a quick lunch with other moms. We also take turns getting grown-up takeout and eating together at our houses where we have safe places for the kids to play."

"You should write a book about this."

"I don't have time to write books. E is for exercise. I get a lot of exercise just working with the vines and so on, but I also jog around the ranch with Jack in the jogger stroller when the weather cooperates. We got really big wheels for it so I can go off-road. Now that there's snow on the ground I put him in a backpack and go snowshoeing. P is for playdates. Playdates are essential two or three times a week. Rotate them around so the kids don't get tired of the same old places or friends. Don't get boring."

"And what's F?"

"Fun. At least once a month I do something

that's just for me. And I mean just for me. Not for Rob, not for Jack. Something I adore. I trade babysitting with a friend, or leave Jack with Rob and give him my full approval to do the same thing." She took another sip of her tea.

Sunshine did the same. "You didn't mention couple time. Don't all the manuals say you have to go on dates with your significant other?"

Morgan blushed. "That's not really a problem for Rob and me. We build in couple time without thinking about it. Maybe we'll have to worry about that later."

Sunshine was jealous, even though she and Cole had been that way too until just a few days ago. Now the chasm between them yawned wide.

"Glepf. I'll remember that… when I have kids."

"Let's put it into play right now."

"What do you mean?"

"I'll take you to today's Moms and Tots meeting. It's a potluck lunch at my friend Gwen's house."

Sunshine glanced at the clock. "That sounds great, as long as you can give me a ride afterward." She explained about the ranch. By the time she was done, Morgan's eyes gleamed with interest.

"That's so great. Cole's going to be out of his mind with happiness on Christmas morning. I want to help."

"Thanks. I'd really appreciate that." Sunshine bit back her desire to tell her about Carl's offer and confess all her doubts. Would she even own the ranch on Christmas morning? Would she and Cole still be together?

They had to be. With or without the property.

"We better get going. Come on. Let's grab Jack and say good-bye to the men."

COLE WAS RELIEVED to find the plumbing problem fixed and the smell dissipated when he returned to the restaurant later that afternoon with Rob. He'd spent most of the day helping Rob with his chores in return for Rob helping him. Ethan arrived soon after they did, along with Jamie.

"The place looks great," Ethan said.

Cole scratched his head. "You mean it doesn't look awful. There's a world of difference between the two."

"Well, it's a little dated."

"A lot dated," Jamie said frankly. "The last time I remember this place open we were just kids. Hasn't it been used for storage ever since?"

"That's what I heard," Cole said. "Seems a shame, given the location."

"Sunshine'll bring new life to it. How much work do you want to do before Christmas?" Ethan asked.

"Won't Sunshine have strong views about what it should look like?" Rob put in.

"She will, but luckily I have this." Cole whipped out a magazine he'd rolled up and stuck in his back pocket earlier. It was already open to a page Sunshine had marked months ago and left on the bed in one of the countless hotels they'd stayed at during their trip.

Cole had stolen it, the idea to purchase her a restaurant in Chance Creek springing fully formed into his mind. "This is what it needs to look like. I won't be able to order the furnishings in time, but I want the rest of it all prepped and ready to go."

Jamie whistled. "Wow. That's going to take a lot of work." They all examined the sleek, modern look of the restaurant in the magazine spread.

"I know. We'd better get started."

"OH MY GOODNESS," Morgan said suddenly, dropping her scrub brush into the bucket. "It's past six o'clock. We're late!"

"After six?" Sunshine scrambled to her feet and wondered why Cole hadn't called to see where she was. Normally he would have.

Maybe he was still mad.

She'd be forever grateful to Morgan for tackling the main bathroom, and to Claire who'd stopped by with a color scheme she'd loved and made to-do lists for the whole renovation project, categorized by room.

"We usually eat right at six. I'd better grab some takeout on the way home. And we still have to pick up Jack. Autumn is a saint."

Autumn had agreed to take Jack while they worked. Still unsure of her final decision about the place, Sunshine felt guilty about letting everyone pitch in to help, but she knew if she decided to move ahead with the project she had too little time to waste any of it.

"I'm so sorry." Sunshine raced to gather up the cleaning supplies while Morgan put the little sample cans of paint Claire had brought on the counter.

"You've got paint in your hair," she called out as Sunshine passed her.

Sunshine rushed to the bathroom, saw that she had a spattering of yellow in her hair from when they'd painted patches of color on the wall to test them, and ducked her head under the tap to scrub it out.

Damp, disheveled and out of breath, she joined Morgan in the car a few minutes later and they drove as quickly as was safe on the snowy roads through the dark streets of Chance Creek, stopping first at the Cruz ranch to pick up Jack and then at the Burger Shack to get dinner.

"Is Rob going to be mad?"

"Are you kidding?" Morgan laughed. "I never

let him get takeout. He'll be over the moon."

Sunshine wondered if Cole would still be giving her the formal treatment, but when they finally reached Morgan's house, both men seemed more distracted than anything.

"Sorry we're late. I picked up some dinner." Morgan tossed the bags of burgers on the table, stripped off her coat and got to work on unzipping Jack's.

"My favorite!" Rob attacked the bags like he hadn't eaten in a month. Morgan shot Sunshine a look that said, *See what I mean?*

Sunshine had to grin despite the tension that had gripped her most of the day. Carl's offer had played in her mind over and over again. She'd thought over her options so many times her head was spinning. All she wanted was a hot bath and to fall into bed.

"Good ol' American takeout." Cole fell on his food with almost as much fervor as Rob did. "You can't get anything like it in Europe. Even at the places that are supposed to be American chains."

Sunshine rolled her eyes. "I didn't let him eat at any of them," she told Morgan. "I was too busy taking him to the best restaurants Europe has to offer."

"Men." Morgan ruffled Rob's hair as she carried Jack over to his high chair. She got out a small container from the fridge and put it in the microwave. A few seconds later, she took it out again and dished out small pieces of meat and mashed potatoes onto a plate for him. Jack grinned when she put it on the tray of his high chair.

"Where were you?" Rob asked.

"And why are you wet?" Cole glanced up as he took another bite of his burger.

Sunshine finally managed to peel off her coat and gloves. She washed her hands at the kitchen sink and joined him and Rob at the table. "Just... playing with my hair."

"She needed a new style," Morgan improvised, feeding Jack.

Cole raised an eyebrow. "Looks exactly the same as it did when you left. Except wet."

"It didn't work, so I took it out again."

"Women," Rob said, leaning back in his chair and reaching out to ruffle Morgan's hair.

"Weren't you in town? Isn't that why you got takeout?" Cole asked.

"Uh..." Sunshine thought fast. "Actually... we were with Autumn."

Both men stopped eating. "Ethan said Autumn was watching Jack." Rob put down his burger and wiped his hands on a napkin.

"She was," Morgan said quickly. "For part of the time."

"So where were you when she was watching Jack?" Cole asked.

"At… Claire's," Sunshine said. Really—what was with the third degree? Couldn't the men just eat their food?

"Jamie said Claire had gone out," Cole said. He put down his burger too. Both men's expressions told her they were caught up in the puzzle.

"We weren't there the whole time," Morgan said.

"You're hiding something," Rob said to her, leaning back in his chair. "That's your hiding-something face. What gives, woman?"

"It's Christmas. I have secrets." She popped the last bite into Jack's mouth, wiped him with a napkin and put the plate on the counter.

"Nope." Rob wouldn't let it go. "That's not your Christmas present face, that's your 'I'm doing something I'm not supposed to do face.'"

Morgan flashed a helpless look at Sunshine. Cole looked from one woman to the other and his expression grew grim. "What's going on? Sunshine?"

"Nothing."

"Baloney. Spill it."

Sunshine panicked. Cole rarely got stern. When he did, it flustered her. "We… we…" Her mind was blank. What could she say they'd been doing? She needed to throw Cole completely off her trail. "We… formed a rock band," she blurted and immediately wished she hadn't. A rock band? Where had that come from? She stammered on, "We were practicing, okay? Do you have any more questions or can you leave well enough alone for once? Because I don't want to talk about it."

You could have heard a pin drop in the stunned silence that followed her outburst.

"We weren't going to tell you about it because we don't want anyone to know," Morgan suddenly said. She grabbed a banana, peeled it and sliced it into rounds with a knife. Placing them on the high chair tray, she washed her hands and joined them at the table.

"Because we aren't any good right now," Sunshine added. "But we will be. Soon. Probably good enough to go on tour."

Morgan frowned. She opened her mouth and closed it again.

Both men stared at them like they'd lost their minds.

Which they had, apparently.

"A band? Do you even play an instrument?" Cole asked slowly.

"Yes." Sunshine was affronted. "I'm awesome at guitar." She knew three chords. Sort of.

The men looked to Morgan.

"Tambourine." She fluttered her hand back and forth. "It's a skill."

Jamie rubbed a hand over his mouth. "When do we get to hear you play?" he asked finally.

"Never," both women said at once.

"Well, maybe someday," Sunshine said. "When we're on tour. But not anytime soon."

After a long moment, Cole shook his head. "If you're so good, I don't think you should hide your talents. I think you should give a Christmas performance, don't you, Rob? You two can pull at least one song together by then, can't you?" He raised a challenging eyebrow and Sunshine quailed. She knew that look. He wasn't going to back down.

She didn't even have a guitar—hadn't owned one in a decade at least. "I... guess," she faltered.

"Good. Can't wait to hear you. Christmas Eve should be a good time for you two to play— when we're all together at Ethan's place."

Chapter Five

COLE COULDN'T BELIEVE Sunshine thought she was fooling anyone. A rock band? Please.

The two women were obviously up to something, and Morgan especially looked guilty as hell.

So did Sunshine.

He didn't like this one bit. Rob was right; if this was about Christmas, Sunshine would have laughed the whole thing off and told him to quit fishing. She was up to something that went much further than a simple gift, and he wanted to know what she was planning. If only he didn't need to spend so much time at the restaurant, he could have followed her the next time she went out, but he'd already planned to meet his friends in town the following day.

He'd have to ferret it out of her tonight.

Before he could continue his line of questioning, however, Sunshine went on the attack.

"Where were *you* this afternoon?" she asked

suddenly and pointed toward the back door. "The snow on your boots hasn't even melted yet. You must have gotten in minutes before we did."

Fuck.

He was careful not to look at Rob, who'd just taken another bite of his burger, but out of the periphery of his vision he saw his friend duck his head guiltily. Cole hoped like hell Rob didn't give him away. "We weren't anywhere in particular," he said at the same time Rob blurted, "We went out for a ride."

"On horseback? In this weather?" Morgan looked from one to the other. "It's been dark for nearly two hours."

"We were slow putting the horses away." Rob dropped the remains of his burger on his plate and went to grab a beer from the fridge.

"It took you two hours to put away the horses?"

"There's always lots of chores." Rob sat down again.

Sunshine was shaking her head. "No, your truck was warm when we walked by. I saw steam rising from it, didn't you, Morgan?"

"That's right. So where were you two?" Morgan demanded.

"It wasn't just the two of them. They said they talked to Ethan. And Jamie." Sunshine narrowed her eyes. "What were you four up to?"

"Just..." Rob waved a hand, but couldn't

seem to come up with an answer.

Cole needed to fill the gap. "Man stuff."

"What kind of man stuff?"

"Just... stuff." Cole couldn't come up with an answer, either. "You know."

"No, I don't. That's why I asked." She wasn't going to let it go and Colt knew that every second he hesitated would make Sunshine more suspicious. He needed to say something concrete. Something that would distract her.

"Just... practicing." Shit, that wasn't what he meant to say.

"Practicing what?" If he'd wanted to distract her, it had worked, but not the way he wanted. She settled in, waiting to hear more.

Cole searched his mind for something— anything—to fill in that blank. Sunshine raised an eyebrow like he had when he'd grilled her. "Practicing..." His mind flipped through possibilities and discarded them one after another. Baseball? Too snowy. Archery? Ditto. What the hell were they practicing?

"Line dancing," Rob blurted.

Cole sent his friend a disgusted look. Sunshine blinked. Then smiled a *gotcha* smile. Now they were well and truly trapped.

It was Morgan who spoke. "Why would you be line dancing?"

"It's... a surprise," Rob squeaked.

Cole wanted to bang his head against the table. Line dancing? That was the most idiotic thing he'd ever heard.

"Well, that's pretty interesting," Morgan said, obviously not buying it for a second. "In fact, I think you all should join our Christmas performance. You can do your dance after we play our song."

"I… don't think that's a good idea." Cole looked to Rob for help, but Rob had popped up again and was searching the refrigerator for… something. Cole didn't know what, and he had an urge to boot his friend and slam the door shut on him. Some help he'd turned out to be.

"Too late," Sunshine said sharply. "If we have to play, you have to dance." She grabbed a packaged salad from the takeout bag, and sailed out of the kitchen into the living room.

"Where are you going?" Cole called after her.

"To watch TV. I'm pooped."

"Me, too," Morgan said. She grabbed the remainder of the fast food and followed Sunshine into the other room.

"Well, now what the hell are we going to do?" Rob asked.

There was nothing for it. "I guess we're going to learn how to dance."

SUNSHINE COULD BARELY keep her eyes open as she sat in front of the television. Her body ached from the unusual activity of working on the house, she was still hungry despite the salad she'd eaten, and she'd never felt so alienated from Cole.

This new trick he was playing cut her to the quick. Bad enough what he'd said about not wanting children. Now he was lying, too?

And he was definitely lying. Line dancing?

No way in hell. Not her fiancé. He knew the same basic set of steps it seemed everyone in the west learned as teenagers, but that was as far as he got. He sure wouldn't spend hours with his friends coming up with a new routine.

So what was he hiding?

Or *who*?

Fran's sharp features filled her mind, along with her cleavage threatening to spill out of her suit jacket. Is that where he'd gone? To see his old girlfriend?

Bitter jealousy curled its fist in her chest. He'd better not have.

She realized it had been weeks since they'd even discussed setting a date for their wedding. Had he lost interest?

She wanted to slink off to their room, but Sunshine stayed in the living room and watched show after inane show on the television, even after Morgan went to put Jack to bed and Rob followed her soon after. Cole went upstairs not long after Rob did, but Sunshine didn't want to face him, so she stayed downstairs.

Around ten she gave up, turned off the TV and the lights and made her way carefully up to the guest room on the second floor. She'd hoped Cole would already be asleep, but a light shone under the door.

Sunshine sighed.

When she opened it, Cole was stretched out on the bed, his clothes still on. He was reading a paperback he must have found on the shelf near the window.

"I'm going to bed," she said, and went to open her suitcase.

"Sounds good." His voice was even, but he didn't sound happy.

Well, neither was she.

They got ready with little more talk and slid under the bedclothes silently. Cole shut off his bedside lamp. "Night."

"Night."

She thought about reaching out to him. Surely one hug could make all the trouble between them disappear.

Fran's face flashed into her mind again and she found she couldn't do it.

She curled on her side and tried to fall asleep.

"I NEVER IN a million years thought I'd see bison in Chance Creek," Cole said the next day, as he leaned on the fence that penned in several of the giant beasts. He'd said good-bye to Rob first thing that morning before making his way to the Mortimers' place. He'd asked him to keep his secret. Rob had promised to do so.

"Aren't they beautiful?" Evan Mortimer said. "Just think what it must have been like in the days when herds stretched for miles."

"A sight to behold."

"Bison meat is making a comeback. I supply restaurants all over Montana now. Bison aren't nearly as hard on the environment as cattle are."

"That's terrific. And you said it was Jake's idea to start a herd?"

"His wife, Hannah's, actually. She rescued a bison that was going to be hunted." He used finger quotations around the word. "There wasn't any real hunting going on, though. Some guy paid a bundle to shoot it in a pen. Hannah set the animal free before that could happen."

"Wow."

"Yeah, wow." Evan chuckled. "The women around here..." He didn't finish the thought.

Cole wished Sunshine knew more of the women in town. He was glad she'd met Autumn, Claire and Morgan, but it took more than a quick visit to make the kind of friendships women seemed to require. "You met Bella during a reality television show?"

"That's right." Evan looked sheepish. "I needed a wife—fast. My assistant convinced me it was a good idea."

"Guess she was right."

"In the end she was, but it was a hell of a fight. Bella gave me a real run for my money." He made a face. "She ended up winning, actually. She got the money she needed to expand her veterinary practice and animal shelter and since we've been married, we've pooled our funds to do all kinds of projects together."

"Someday soon I hope to have land," Cole said, wondering if he'd made a huge mistake buying the restaurant for Sunshine. The way things were going she'd never cook there. Maybe he should have been selfish and bought a ranch instead. Well, he still would, come hell or high water. "I need to make a plan for how best to use it. Any suggestions? Maybe bison?"

"Maybe. You'd need a big spread, though. Bison require a lot of grazing room. Have you considered windmills?"

"No, can't say I have." He pictured the big wooden tourist traps he and Sunshine had seen in Holland, but he figured Evan meant something more modern.

"I've heard some ranchers make more money selling green energy back to the power companies from wind turbines than they make by traditional methods these days. I plan to bring some in soon. I'm also studying German farm and ranch practices. They create power from manure and composting, too. They're way ahead of us in efficiency and energy production."

"Huh." He'd never given windmills a thought, but it made sense. "Thanks, I'll look into that."

"Let's get together again soon and talk about it. Maybe we can help each other with research, or get some kind of discount if we buy them together."

"Sounds great. Listen, I need to head into town." He described the restaurant he'd bought for Sunshine and his plans for it. "The contractors are coming today to work on the floor. I'd like to be there to supervise."

Evan looked at his watch. "I can join you for a while. You can put me to work—how's that?"

"I'd appreciate it. But I'd like to go before Sunshine gets here."

"I think you're too late," Evan said, bringing Cole back to the present. "That looks like Morgan's car coming up the drive."

"Don't say a word to her," Cole cautioned him.

"I won't. I'll tell her you're helping me with an errand in town. Can't ruin a Christmas surprise."

He led the way back up toward the house to meet Morgan and Sunshine. Cole made the introductions between them, and Bella came out of her veterinary practice to say hello.

Cole was ready to make excuses for their departure when Bella invited Sunshine to tour her practice and the kennels. Morgan said her good-byes and a few minutes later, Cole and Evan were able to slip into Evan's truck without being seen.

When they reached the restaurant, Ethan and Jamie were already there, as was the contractor whose job it was to sand down and refinish the hardwood floor in the dining area. While the contractor and his assistants got busy on that job, the men swarmed over the large kitchen, scrubbing every appliance, cupboard and counter. Cole had decided that the functional stainless steel appliances would stay. They didn't need to be swapped out like the furniture and decorations in the dining room. Several hours later, he judged that they were a third of the way done. He thanked the other men and sent them on their way, knowing they all had chores to do. "Remember, you were line dancing," he told them on their way out.

"Autumn will never believe that," Ethan said.

"Neither will Claire. I'm going to keep my mouth shut," Jamie said.

"You'd better. If you spill the beans you'll ruin everything," Cole said.

But he had a feeling things had already been ruined.

"YOU'VE NEVER OWNED a dog?" Bella asked

Sunshine in disbelief as they toured her animal shelter. "Not even as a kid?"

"My parents weren't animal people," she explained, her mind still on Cole and how awkward things were between them. "And when I moved out I worked a lot. There just wasn't time or space for a pet."

"Well, I'm a sucker for animals. I couldn't do without them." Bella led the way further into the large building. Sunshine expected to see rows of cages, and there were separate places for all the different animals, but there were also plenty of spaces for the pets to be together—big spaces with different types of terrain and obstacles that the animals could explore. Several young adults were working in the shelter, too, some cleaning cages and dishing out food to the animals and others exercising and playing with them.

"This is amazing," Sunshine said, taking in the scope of the building. "Oh, my goodness, there are so many."

"We take in overflow from other shelters. We're able to subsidize spaying and neutering and have a very progressive adoption program. It's a lot to handle, though, now that I'm pregnant."

"Pregnant?" Sunshine cast a sideways look at Bella's flat belly. "How far along are you? This looks like a lot of hard work."

"It is, but I have help, and I'm not due until

July. Another vet is coming in to take over for the first three months after my baby is born. After that I'll be right back to work. I'm looking for a live-in nanny and housekeeper."

Sunshine wished she could afford help like that. The Mortimers were obviously well off if the log-house style mansion she'd seen when they drove in was anything to go by. She squashed a surge of jealousy. She'd traveled the world, after all, and by buying the ranch she was investing the rest of her money in something worthwhile.

She didn't have time to wonder once again if she should sell to Carl; there was far too much to look at. When they entered the area where one of the volunteers was playing with several dogs, a large, shaggy yellow mutt bounded up and gave its paw to Sunshine.

"That's Duke," Bella said. "He's a wonderful dog. I've only had him a week and haven't put him up on our adoption website yet. I know the minute I do he'll get snapped up. He's a happy, healthy, loving animal that's just right for a family."

Sunshine shook the dog's paw and let go, but Duke didn't bound away. Instead he sat down in front of her and whined, as if asking for something.

"What is it, boy?" Sunshine asked. When the dog whined again, she knelt down to take a closer look at him, thinking maybe he was hurt, but that made no sense; Bella was a vet. Still, Sunshine couldn't ignore his doggy pleas. "What's wrong?" She pet him a few times and Duke's joy was unmistakeable. His tail thumped on the ground and when he couldn't restrain himself anymore, he licked her face.

Sunshine rubbed his fur and his tail thumped harder. Her attentions made him so happy, she finally plunked down on her bottom and wrapped her arms around his neck. Duke nuzzled her and his tail thumped even harder.

"Have you two met before?" Bella laughed. "This is starting to look like a reunion."

"More like a reunion of kindred spirits," Sunshine said. Bella was right; she felt like she knew Duke already—like she was greeting a long-lost friend. She knew instinctively that this dog was prepared to love her wholeheartedly for the rest of its life.

"Maybe you should adopt him."

"Oh, I couldn't." Not the way things were. Even discounting the fact that the new home she'd bought needed renovation and she was pregnant, she wasn't sure about her relationship with Cole.

And then there was Carl, who'd called her again. She'd put him off another couple of days.

"Why not?" Bella looked curious, not challenging.

"Because… I don't know." Sunshine rubbed her cheek against Duke's fur, unwilling to express her fears.

"Don't tell me you're not staying." Bella sounded upset.

Sunshine looked up in surprise. "Would it affect you if I went?"

"It would affect everyone I know. People talk about you two all the time."

"Really?" She hadn't realized that. She'd miss Chance Creek and its inhabitants if she left, but if she and Cole broke up she wouldn't be able to stay here. Seeing him all the time with someone else would kill her. "Anyway, I don't plan to leave." Yet, she added silently, then gave herself a mental shake. She and Cole were far from splitting up. She was being overdramatic. Time to change the subject. "Can you keep a secret?"

"Of course."

As Sunshine filled Bella in about the ranch and her efforts to spruce it up, Bella's eyes shone. "I have an idea." She bit her lip. "Or maybe not. I don't want to offend you."

"How would you offend me?"

"It's just… Evan inherited a bunch of furniture last month from his great uncle. A lot of it was pretty great, so we've integrated it into our house, which means we have too many of everything. I've got extra couches and chairs and tables. All of it is practically new. I don't want it to go to waste. Do you want to look through it and see if any of it works?"

"Sure. That sounds great. But how will I transport it without Evan learning where it went? None of the men can know until Christmas morning. They couldn't keep a secret from Cole."

"We'll figure out something." Bella watched Sunshine pet Duke. "So I heard a funny rumor. Something about you starting a rock band?"

"Oh, lord. Are you serious?" Rob must have said something.

"I'm dying to know what that's all about."

As Sunshine recounted what had happened, Bella snorted.

"It's not funny," Sunshine said, getting to her feet.

"Yes, it is. But you know what? I've actually got a couple of guitars. I've taken some lessons."

"I took a few, too. I know just enough to be dangerous."

"So let's practice later. We can figure out a song."

Sunshine shrugged. "Why the hell not? I don't suppose you have a tambourine."

"No, but we'll order one tonight. Express mail." She patted Duke's head. "Tell you what. I'll hold onto Duke for a week, too. That will give you a chance to think things over. If you can't take him, I'll put him up for adoption then."

"I don't want you to waste your time…"

"Are you kidding? I love this dog. I'm not in any hurry to let him go." Bella grinned. "Of course, I can say that for all the rest of the pets in the shelter, too."

"You really are obsessed with animals."

"Hey, I said I was a sucker for them, not obsessed."

"Is there a difference?" Sunshine grinned back at Bella. It was hard to be depressed around her optimism and can-do attitude. "You know, I think I could get obsessed, too." She nearly melted when she spotted a passel of kittens stumbling around one of the pens in the cat area.

"My suggestion is to come volunteer for me rather than getting knee deep in critters yourself."

"That sounds like a good idea."

Chapter Six

COLE WAS PLEASED to see that Sunshine was in a better mood at dinner, which Bella and Evan served in their elegant dining room. When he'd come home late again he'd found her taking a nap in the bedroom Bella had assigned them, something he'd rarely seen her do before. He'd been worried; she looked exhausted, but when he woke her up she claimed she'd only been resting her eyes for a few minutes.

Now she laughed at Bella and Evan's jokes and she'd eaten two helpings of the vegetarian chili and cornbread Bella had whipped up.

"This is good practice for me," Bella told them. "Evan's whole extended family is arriving in town for Christmas and I've never hosted such a large group of people. I want to make sure I know what I'm doing. We always eat in the kitchen."

"We'll gladly be your guinea pigs," Sunshine told her.

"Everything is vegan, including dessert," Bella announced. "Morgan told me about your preferences, Sunshine."

"Oh, I hope you didn't go to a lot of trouble."

"No, that was good practice, too. One of Evan's cousins prefers gluten-free food, another is vegetarian and a third is doing the Paleo diet."

Sunshine laughed. "That's a tricky combination."

"But I'm determined to pull it off. And I've got all kinds of activities and games planned. You should see all the holiday decorations I still have to put up. I actually hand-sewed a bunch of them." Bella smiled sheepishly. "I'm not sure where this rush of domesticity is coming from. Maybe it's the pregnancy."

"Maybe." Sunshine took another bite of cornbread. It was delicious.

"I hope when Sunshine gets pregnant, she gets a similar rush," Cole said as he helped himself to another serving of chili.

Sunshine snapped her head around to stare at him. "Two days ago you said you didn't want kids," she said dryly.

"What? I never said that," he lied. He knew exactly what she meant, but it wasn't fair for her to bring it up like that. He'd said what he'd said in the heat of the moment. Maybe Sunshine didn't realize that, though.

Sunshine looked like she'd say more, but instead she changed the subject. Cole hoped she hadn't taken his hasty words to heart. He'd always wanted to be a dad. He just figured they'd sort out the details after they were married.

Halfway through dessert Sunshine's cell phone rang. To Cole's surprise, she put a hand in her pocket and turned off the ringer without answering it.

"Aren't you going to get that?"

"Not at dinner."

"Oh, don't worry about us. We're not formal," Bella said. "By the way, Cab Johnson called. He and Rose would love to put you folks up tomorrow night. He sounded put out you hadn't stopped by to see him yet, Cole."

"I'll call him right after dinner. Why don't you get that call, honey," he said to Sunshine. "It could be your folks." He was beginning to feel guilty that he hadn't suggested they spend Christmas with Sunshine's family. He knew she missed them. He felt bad he hadn't gone to see Cab, either. He was letting too much slide.

Sunshine bit her lip, pulled out the phone and looked at the screen. She got up from her seat before answering it, and left the room.

Cole frowned. Was it his imagination or was she acting secretive? He'd bet anything that wasn't her parents who'd called. Without meaning to, he stood up too and followed her without an explanation to their hosts. Something about Sunshine's manner triggered all his instincts. She was hiding something.

And it wasn't a rock band.

"I haven't made up my mind yet," he heard her say in a low voice when he got close to the billiard room Sunshine had disappeared into. "I don't know. I said I don't know." She broke off and listened. "Because I have a lot to think over. Until I'm sure, I can't answer you." Another pause. "Look, that's all I'm willing to say right now. I know you're in a hurry. I—" She sighed. "Believe me, I know exactly how you feel. I'm right there with you." She waited a beat. "Okay, I'll call you tomorrow if I can. Bye."

Cole hurried back to the table before Sunshine did, sat down and spooned a forkful of food into his mouth. Neither Evan nor Bella seemed to think anything was amiss and no one commented on the call when Sunshine returned. Meanwhile, Cole's thoughts were in turmoil.

Who the hell was she talking to?

Had she met another man?

The evening passed at a crawl and though he could tell he would have enjoyed Evan and Bella's company at any other time, the wait until bedtime was almost unbearable. Cole held it together until he and Sunshine crawled into bed, but when he opened his mouth to question her, she beat him to it.

"Did you ever think about having a dog?"

A dog? Who cared about dogs? "Of course," he ground out. "I love dogs. So who—"

"What kind would you want to get?"

"I don't know. A mutt? Look, Sunshine—"

"What kind of mutt?"

"Any kind!" Cole turned over. "Some big, yellow dog."

"Yellow dog?" She sounded interested.

Cole couldn't believe they were having this conversation. Why was she suddenly so obsessed with dogs? "Yellow dogs are happy dogs. Haven't you noticed?" This wasn't what he wanted to talk about. He needed to confront her. She'd been talking with some stranger, telling him she didn't know—

Cole broke off. She didn't know... what kind of dog to get him?

Was this his Christmas surprise?

He relaxed back into the pillows and almost laughed out loud. No wonder the women looked so damn guilty. They must have been working on his Christmas present. After all, wasn't that exactly what he and his friends were doing? He'd psyched himself out thinking it was something more complicated, but Sunshine hadn't ever had a dog. Maybe she'd gotten her friends together to help her choose one. Maybe they were taking turns caring for it so he wouldn't know. That would explain a lot of things.

"I have noticed that," Sunshine said. "I like yellow dogs, too."

Was she smiling? It sounded like it, but he couldn't see. Relief flooded Cole. Sunshine wasn't cheating on him.

Thank God.

"Cole," she said suddenly. "Did you mean that about children? Do you really want a family? Because I didn't think you did."

He wanted to pull her into a hug. "Yeah, I want a family. Soon. First we need a house, though. I need a job, too. I want to make sure we can do this right." They were treading on shaky ground now, though. He couldn't talk about this stuff without talking about the wedding. That was supposed to be a conversation for Christmas morning. "Like you said before, let's not talk about anything serious until after the holidays."

When she spoke again her voice had gone flat. "Fine with me."

"Hey—"

"You're right; it's no big deal. We'll talk about it some other time."

He propped himself up on one elbow, torn about what to do. He had a whole plan for making Christmas morning special, and if he broached marriage now, it would ruin it. "Sunshine, you know I love you, don't you?"

"I guess." She didn't sound convinced.

"You guess?"

"I don't know. I don't feel like we're on the same page these days."

Alarmed, Cole sat upright. "What page are you on?"

She sat up too. "It's more like what page have you traipsed onto?"

"I haven't *traipsed* anywhere."

"Are you sure you haven't traipsed all over Fran?"

Cole snorted. "Is that what this is about? Fran? That was a hundred years ago. So I slept with her a few times—"

"A few *hundred* times."

"You weren't a virgin when I met you." Cole clamped his mouth shut. Hell. That wasn't going to go over well.

"Are you calling me a slut?" Sunshine scrambled away from him.

"No. Damn it, you know that's not what I—"

She crawled right out of the bed. "Good night, Cole."

"Wait. Sunshine, where are you going? I never said you were a slut—I just said you slept around—"

A pillow whacked him in the face. Cole wasn't sure how Sunshine had managed that. "Very mature."

Sunshine didn't answer. A second later she left the room. Cole ran a hand through his hair and swore. He was just about to pursue her when the door opened again and she came back in.

"I'm not sleeping on a stupid couch, and I don't want to talk any more, you hear?"

"But—"

"One more word and you can go sleep downstairs."

He didn't want to do that and they obviously weren't going to work this out tonight. Cole gave in. It was all this moving around, he told himself as he flopped back down on the mattress. Sunshine climbed back in the bed beside him. As soon as Christmas was over he was going to find them a house if it was the last thing he did. Twenty minutes later, Sunshine's even breathing told him she'd fallen asleep.

He wished he could find that oblivion.

THE MORNING FOUND them packing their bags again to move to Cab and Rose Johnson's house. They did so in silence, broken only by the shortest questions and answers. Sunshine was beginning to feel like they'd gotten stuck on some kind of ride they couldn't get off. Their tempers were worn thin; no wonder they couldn't have a conversation without getting into an argument.

Cole drove her back to the Cruz ranch and left her on the front porch of the small cabin Cab and Rose inhabited. "I'm meeting Cab in town at the Sheriff's station," Cole said. "See you to-night."

Sunshine knocked on the door and watched him drive away. Part of her knew she was being overly sensitive. Last night she'd interpreted everything Cole had said in the worst possible way. Still, he had said it, and it wasn't fair. She'd only had a few serious relationships before she met him. She certainly hadn't slept around.

She liked the looks of Cab and Rose's homey cottage after the huge log cabin Evan and Bella inhabited, though. Evan and Bella had decorated their place beautifully and their guest bedroom had been to die for, but she relaxed when Rose showed her the small bedroom they would occupy for the night.

"I'm sorry it isn't fancier," she said. "We're getting ready to build a home soon, but it won't be done for another year at least."

"I'd be sorry if it was." Sunshine had had enough of fancy. She wanted to get home. Good thing the ranch house was beginning to shape up, even as her relationship with Cole was crashing to the ground. Sunshine wondered if she would end up living there alone. She couldn't think of a worse fate.

She'd known Cab from the days of running her café next to Cole's rifle range. She'd always liked the man's dry humor and no-nonsense personality. Rose complemented him nicely. She ran the jewelry store in town and she was cheerful and caring. Sunshine wondered if the rumors about her sixth sense were true. Bella had told her Rose could sense whether a couple's love would stand the test of time when they came into the store and chose an engagement ring. Cole had bought her engagement ring from Thayer, the former owner. He hadn't been the recipient of any kind of prediction.

Maybe she should be grateful for that.

"I have to open the jewelry store soon. Would you like to come with me and hang out for the morning? I'd love to hear all about your trip. And your rock band," Rose added with a sly smile. "I'm so jealous, you know. I always wanted to sing in a band."

Sunshine flashed her a half-hearted grin. She should have known Rose would have heard about the band. "You're hired! We don't have a singer yet. Bella and I practiced some guitar earlier this morning. We didn't sound half bad."

Actually, Bella had sounded okay. Sunshine had been awful, but after she'd half-memorized the few chords required for the song they'd picked, she'd started to get the hang of it again.

"Awesome. When's your next practice?"

"This afternoon. Think you can get away for an hour?"

"Maybe." Rose glanced at the clock. "We'd better get going." Fifteen minutes later, she unlocked the door to the jewelry store and let Sunshine in. "There are a few things I need to take care of before I open. Make yourself at home."

Sunshine wandered among the glass cases as Rose performed her chores. Looking at the engagement rings, she remembered the Christmas morning Cole had proposed. It had been the happiest day of her life. Surely there was some way to get back to that feeling.

To divert herself, she said, "I can't believe you actually bought this place off of old man Thayer."

"I know. It felt like a miracle at the time. I've come a long way since then, though."

"A lot changed while I was traveling."

"Hasn't it? You missed so many weddings. And babies!" As she continued to talk, Rose turned on more lights and began to put things in order for the day. A moment later, the front door opened and a small, dark-haired woman came in.

"Mia, have you met Sunshine?" Rose asked.

"I don't think so." The petite woman came to shake her hand. She was youthful, with a long ponytail that swished when she walked.

"Mia married Luke Matheson, Rob's brother. She has a wedding-planning business. We share the space," Rose said.

"That sounds like a fun business." Sunshine perked up, thinking of her own wedding, but then remembered how rocky things were at the moment with Cole.

"It is. Hectic, but fun." Mia opened the door to a small office to one side of the large room. "This is my headquarters."

Sunshine peeked in to see a wide desk and shelves of idea books. Every inch of space was in use. It looked more like an artist's studio than a normal office.

"So tell us about your trip," Rose said when they came out into the store again.

Sunshine did so, focusing on all the different types of food she'd learned to prepare and how her journey had affected the way she thought about cooking. She tried to forget her argument with Cole, but she found it hard.

"Are you going to write a cookbook now?" Rose asked.

"I hope you took photographs," Mia said. "That kind of cookbook wouldn't be complete without them."

"Cole took tons of them. We haven't been able to sort through them yet. I need to get into my house first." Or maybe she needed to sell the house and walk away from everything.

A twinge in her abdomen reminded her she was linked to Cole in a way she couldn't ignore.

"I heard you bought a ranch. What's it like?" Rose asked.

Sunshine told them about the ranch and both

of the women exclaimed over the plan. "We'll help any way we can," Mia told her. "We love that kind of thing."

It was hard to drum up the necessary enthusiasm. With each passing minute, she felt more and more like she was making a mistake. Carl really wanted the ranch. She had no idea what she wanted these days. Certainly not a relationship filled with lies and distrust.

"Tell her about the band," Rose said. "I'm going to be lead singer."

"A band? Can I play drums? I'm awesome at drums!"

"Really?" Sunshine hadn't expected that.

"Yes, really." Mia's ponytail swung for emphasis. "Do you have a drummer already?"

Sunshine made an effort to concentrate. "We don't even have drums."

"I can borrow some from a friend. It's not like she ever plays them," Mia said confidently.

Well, that was something. "You can store them out at the house. Bella's bringing our guitars out this afternoon and she's already ordered a tambourine," Sunshine said.

"This is going to be so much fun!"

Sunshine was glad someone was enjoying the prospect. She fought against a wave of nausea and braced herself against a glass showcase, willing her stomach to settle down. She pretended to examine the landscapes that decorated one wall of the showroom.

"Rose is an artist," Mia said, following her gaze. "She's not just good at painting, either. She's terrific at layout and design."

"If you ever want help with your cookbook, just ask. I'd love to help," Rose said.

"I will." Sunshine got the upper hand on her wayward stomach. "I would like to write one. I just don't know where to start."

"With the recipes, of course." Rose smiled. "Pick out all your favorites and then tell the story of where and when you learned how to make them."

Sunshine thought about the naan she'd made in Turkmenistan, the peanut stew she'd made in Ethiopia, and the chili relish she'd made in India. In each case the story revolved around women. Mothers. Mothers cooking for their children and putting all the love and hope and dreams they had for their children's lives into each dish.

She'd kept journals during her trips and those themes came into play over and over again. If she'd learned one thing, it was that the world over, mothers worried themselves sick over their children. Their greatest cares came from raising them, and their greatest triumphs were experienced through them.

Could she write about that in any way that would make sense to other women?

"You two are so lucky you work together,"

she said. She wondered if she'd ever make a friend like that in Chance Creek. When she'd left Chicago, she'd ended up growing apart from the best friend she'd had there. During her time in Chance Creek, she'd gotten somewhat close to Kerri Olsen, who ran a second-hand store in town, but without steady cell phone coverage for the first half of her trip, they'd texted back and forth less and less frequently as the months went by, and she'd lost track of her, too.

Time to give her a call.

Except maybe she'd be leaving again soon.

"We know," Rose said. "We tell each other that all the time."

"I think women need to have friends around when they work," Mia said. "We're social creatures. We think out loud."

"I know I do," Rose said. "I get inspired about something and tell Mia, then she gets inspired and comes up with a better idea, then I riff on that one... We're better together."

"Once you're settled, you can come hang out sometimes. We can put up a table in a corner somewhere and you can write your cookbook."

"I'd like that." Another wave of nausea hit her. It was worse today than it had ever been before. Sunshine had hoped she'd sail through this part without being affected much, but that obviously wasn't going to happen.

"Sunshine? Are you okay?" Rose asked.

"I… I think I'm going to be sick."

Rose rushed her into the back to a small bathroom, pushed her inside and shut the door behind her. Sunshine dropped to her knees and lost the contents of her stomach in the toilet. She retched until there was nothing left and sagged against the wall. This was awful. Could she really survive a month or two of morning sickness?

When she'd cleaned herself up and came out of the bathroom, she knew immediately both women had guessed her secret.

"You're pregnant," Rose said, confirming it.

"Yes."

"Does Cole know?" Mia asked.

Sunshine shook her head. "It's supposed to be a surprise."

Rose surged forward and hugged her. "Congratulations!" Mia quickly followed her.

"Thanks. But I feel so…"

"Awful?" Rose said sympathetically. "The first trimester can be hard."

"You need a lot of rest," Mia said. "And you've been bouncing from house to house. That can't be easy."

"When will your house be ready to move in?" Rose asked.

"I wanted to wait until Christmas morning. It's supposed to be Cole's Christmas present."

"Well, it won't be long now. How much more is there to do?"

"I don't know. Too much."

Mia and Rose exchanged another look. "Do you need help?"

Sunshine was ashamed of herself. "Everyone's helping already. I'm sure you two are busy—"

"Never too busy to help a friend," Rose said.

"Have you talked to Autumn about your cookbook idea?" Mia asked suddenly. "She told me recently that she was getting a cookbook published."

"Really? She didn't say a thing to me."

"Autumn's like that," Mia said. "She'd never toot her own horn."

"You two should get together and brainstorm," Mia put in. "Why don't I see if she can join us for lunch?"

"She's got guests at her B&B," Sunshine protested, but it was too late. Before she knew it Mia had made the call, and when Autumn said she couldn't make lunch, but she could do tea later on, Mia called Fila Matheson and Camila Torres and invited them, too.

"Why not get all the great cooking minds together in one place?" she said. "Besides, you need some female friends if you're going to settle in Chance Creek."

"That sounds like a good idea." Sunshine just hoped she'd be here long enough to enjoy them.

COLE APPRECIATED THE fact that the sheriff had made time for him this morning. He knew his job was a busy one and Cab probably had more than his share of problems on his plate.

"Don't you need to work?" he said when Cab offered to take him for a drive around town to show him what had changed during his absence.

"I'm not on duty this morning; I just came in to do some paperwork. Besides, I like to cruise around in my own truck from time to time and take a look at things. You'd be surprised what happens in plain sight when people don't know there's a sheriff around."

Cole chuckled. "All right. I'll ride along and keep my eyes peeled for trouble."

"Got any plans now you're back?" Cab asked when they'd been on the road for a few minutes. Cole enjoyed looking out the window. It was good to be home.

"A few."

"What about the shooting range? Ready to take it back?"

"You're not the first to ask that question. Just curious or is there more to it?" Cole watched a woman clearing the latest fall of snow off her Chevrolet.

"Scott's done a good job, hasn't he?"

Cole felt a pang. He'd talked to Scott on the phone when he'd first arrived, but he'd been so busy with the restaurant, he hadn't even stopped by yet to see the man. He promised himself he'd go to the range tomorrow and see Scott in person. He focused on Cab's question. "He's done great."

"Seems like a good business for him."

"Has Scott been talking about wanting to buy? Because again—you're not the first person to mention that."

Cab drove with the precision of a man used to being behind the wheel. "He hasn't said anything in so many words. But he had a rough go of it in the past and I think he's thriving now. Seems like he's kept those rentals in line, too."

"Sure has. Rents are up."

"If you're not dying to get back into either business…"

"…it makes sense to sell," Cole finished for him. "I know. Problem is, I haven't figure out what to do instead."

"Really?"

The look Cab shot him told Cole the sheriff knew more than he should.

"Hell," Cole said. "Who spilled the beans?"

"I've got my fingers in a lot of pies," Cab said. "You bought yourself a restaurant. Aren't you and Sunshine going to run it?"

"Sunshine is. I'm no cook, you know that." He tried to shake his unease over the fight he and Sunshine had the previous evening, but he failed miserably. He didn't know why they were arguing all the time.

Cab chuckled in agreement. "Thought you might have learned in your fancy trip around the world."

"I mostly ate whatever Sunshine made. Since I've been home I've been nosing around to see what other options I have, but I've come up empty." Cole filled him in on everything he'd learned and Cab nodded, as if unsurprised.

"It's all about finding a niche that hasn't been filled," he said. "I'll keep my ears and eyes open, but you know who you should talk to? Jake. I know he wants to talk to you, too. We've got family coming to stay tomorrow, so how about I give him a call and see if you can spend a night at his place. Jake's pretty entrepreneurial, and he's got connections. You heard about him and Evan and the bison, right?"

"Definitely. Jake's at school these days, though. Doesn't Evan run the operation?"

"For now, but really he's the investor. As soon as Jake returns from school for good, he'll take it over again. He's the one to talk to. Meanwhile, how about we go poke a stick at your restaurant? I hear it's shaping up nicely."

"That sounds good. I'm supposed to meet some guys there anyway."

When they reached the restaurant, Cole was gratified to find the floors finished. The whole place was coming together. With the old booths removed, the space was far more open and modern.

"You'll take dining in Chance Creek to a whole new level with this place," Cab said.

"I hope Sunshine likes it."

"So what's this I hear about line dancing?"

Cole flushed. "Hell, people are talking about that?"

"Nothing stays a secret in Chance Creek. Are you really taking lessons?"

"Oh, it's worse than that," Jamie said. He'd just come into the restaurant, followed by Rob. "We're all supposed to be taking lessons."

"I can't wait to see the performance Christmas Eve." Cab was enjoying this too much for Cole's comfort.

"Hell, you've seen this place," Rob said. "That means you're in the performance, too."

"I don't think so." The big man held up his hands as if to fend that thought off.

"That's the rule. Anyone who walks through that door is in on the game, which means they have to cover their tracks. You're going to need lessons," Jamie said.

"I'm a good dancer. I don't need lessons," Cab protested.

Cole laughed along with the others. "Don't worry, we've got an instructor coming by later. We just need to learn one dance, after all."

"I notice you didn't tell me that rule before

you invited me over here." Cab crossed his arms over his chest.

The sheriff might have intimidated other men, but Cole had known him for years. "You invited yourself over," he pointed out. "Anyway, I didn't want to spoil the surprise." He ducked when Cab took a swing at him. "Come on; it's all for a good cause."

"What cause is that?"

"My relationship."

Cole hadn't meant to say that, but now it was out and the men surrounding him regarded him with surprise. "Something wrong between you and Sunshine?" Jamie asked.

Cole didn't really want to talk about it, but he found himself answering the question. "She's been acting weird lately. I don't know if she even wants to get married anymore."

"That sounds serious," Cab said. "Have you asked her?"

"To set a date? Not yet. I'm saving that for Christmas." He crossed to the plate-glass window and stared out at the street. Maybe he'd be too late.

"I mean about your relationship. Have you asked her if something's changed?" Cab said, following him.

"No."

"Why not?"

"Because if it has, I don't want to know."

SUNSHINE STRETCHED HER aching muscles. The good news was that her nausea seemed to disappear late in the afternoon. The bad news was that once it did, she was more aware of her muscles. Her friends kept pressing her not to do much work, and with their help she didn't have to, but it was her house she was renovating. She wanted to pitch in and do her share.

Especially since she might turn around and sell it again.

The more she cleaned the place, the more she fell in love with it, though. She wanted to furnish every nook and corner. She knew it was silly, but she felt that the home wanted her here—and wanted her to fill it with a family.

But houses weren't alive.

And she had to make a sensible choice.

Her meeting with the other chefs in town had been fun, but not as informative as she suspected Rose had hoped. Autumn had brought Arianna along and Mia had Pam. Between the two of them, the chatter among the women had been punctuated by squeals and shrieks and toddlers running amok in the restaurant. At least she'd managed to tell Autumn, Fila and Camila about the rock band. All three women asked to join in, Autumn on guitar, and Camila and Fila as singers. Autumn promised to fill Claire in on this development, too, mentioning that Claire knew how to play the piano. They had a good laugh at the lengths Sunshine was willing to go to in order to keep Cole's Christmas present a secret, but unfortunately things got chaotic soon afterward.

Autumn had done her best to explain about her cookbook contract to Sunshine, but she'd barely started to talk when Arianna bumped her head on the table and broke into shrieks. A few minutes later, Pam managed to spill a glass of water. All Sunshine had learned from Fila and Camila during the noisy aftermath was that their business was booming. That made her even less confident than before—Chance Creek wasn't that big a town. If people loved Fila's, was there room for another restaurant?

It was disconcerting to watch the other women try to corral their children, too. She must be crazy if she thought she could balance any kind of work and motherhood.

Again and again she pictured Carl with a fist-ful of money. With it, she could do anything she wanted.

She was so preoccupied with her thoughts, she slipped into bed beside Cole that night, snuggled close to him and gave him a kiss. Only his surprised intake of breath reminded her they were fighting.

Before she could pull away, he wrapped an arm around her, pulled her close and kissed her back, a kiss so hungry she melted under it, despite everything.

"Cole—"

"No. Don't try to figure it out. Not tonight."
He kissed her again.

He was right, Sunshine realized. If they tried
to talk things out they'd probably make it worse,
judging by the last few days, and she needed him
as much as he needed her. She'd missed Cole's
strong arms around her. His mouth on hers
made her come alive for the first time in days.
With a sigh, she acquiesced and he pulled her
even closer.

Letting their bodies talk for them was probably the smartest thing they'd done in weeks,
Sunshine thought fleetingly a few minutes later.
Cole's hands stroking her skin had already stoked
the desire in her veins. She moved with him, her
fingers tracing the muscles of his shoulders, his
back, and slipping downward to urge him inside
of her.

But Cole wasn't having that. He dipped
down to take one of her nipples in his mouth
and Sunshine arched her back, wanting more. As
his tongue teased her, desire blossomed inside
her all over again. After all the time they'd spent
together in just this way, her interest in Cole's
body never diminished. The touch of him and
taste of him swirled together into a cocktail of
lust that heated her and made her hungry for him
again and again.

Cole settled himself between her thighs and

nudged them open with his legs. Sunshine let him take charge, glorying in the sensations he was calling forth from her body. It was such a sweet mystery to her how two people coming together added up to so much more than themselves. Where did these feelings come from, and how could they take over like this, making everything else so unimportant?

For a second, her worries came back—could Cole possibly sense her pregnancy? She'd already seen changes in her breasts when she looked in the mirror, and they were sensitive tonight. Would Cole notice the difference in the dark?

He didn't seem to, and she relaxed again, moaning when he slid down and kissed a trail between her breasts, down her stomach and lower still.

Sunshine's fingers tangled in the sheets as his tongue did wicked things to her innermost core. Her breath sped up and her hips lifted of their own accord until she was so close to losing control she whimpered a warning to Cole.

He understood and moved over her until he covered her once more. Sometimes he asked her if she was ready. Not tonight. She knew why— any words between them could break this spell.

Neither of them wanted that.

As he sank into her, she pushed up to welcome him, and a sweet ache lanced through her chest as her heart embraced the truth she hadn't been able to see these past few days.

She loved Cole.

Loved him.

A few harsh words, a misunderstanding—nothing like that would ever come between them. He loved her, too. She knew that with all her heart and soul. Fran—she nearly laughed. Fran was a ridiculous episode from his past.

So why was she trying to use the woman to add fuel to the flames of discord between them?

Cole moved inside her with a rhythm she joined instinctively, and she let thought go again, willing to move forward on trust that what felt so right couldn't lead them astray. As Cole increased his pace and the delicious friction between them heated up, she gave herself over to it, letting the tension build up until she crashed over into ecstasy like a wave on the sand. As pleasure pulsed through her again and again, and she felt Cole crash into her in the throes of his own release, Sunshine forgot her body and moved straight into the light and heat they'd built between them.

Nothing but this mattered. Nothing but this was true.

If there was pain in her heart, Cole hadn't put it there.

As Sunshine came back to herself, slack and panting on the bed, still encircled in Cole's arms, she realized it was true: there was pain in her heart, and she'd put it there.

And she was the only one who could get it out again.

Chapter Seven

"SUNSHINE?" HER STILLNESS worried Cole and he braced himself on his elbows, trying not to crush her.

"I love you." Her whisper feathered over him. For some reason her words scared him even more. He sensed a 'but' in there somewhere.

"I love you too."

"I haven't been honest with you."

Cole swallowed in a suddenly dry throat. "Okay." He pulled out and shifted off of her, and Sunshine sat up. He could make out the shape of her, but he couldn't see details. He reached for the light but she stopped him.

"It's about my work."

Cole felt a rush of relief. He could handle anything that had to do with cooking. As long as Sunshine wasn't going to leave him—

He went cold. Was she going to leave him? Was this what the trouble between them was really about?

"I thought I'd made up my mind. I chose Chance Creek, and you, and the idea of having a family."

"But…" He knew it was coming.

"But I'm a chef, Cole. I'm not just a cook, I'm not just an entrepreneur. I'm a chef."

"I know." He did know. Unfortunately, he knew all too well what she was saying. It was why he'd rushed to buy a restaurant here and tried to make it perfect—because deep down he knew what Sunshine needed wasn't in Chance Creek. He'd hoped if he could tie her up with a property and a job, she might forget the rest of her dreams. "So, you want to go back to Chicago." He felt as if something was dying inside him. Ultimately, he wanted to make Sunshine happy. If she wanted to go, he'd go. He sure as hell couldn't watch her walk away.

"No."

Her quiet word didn't sink in at first. "No?" he repeated. Had he heard that right?

"I don't want to go back to Chicago. The thing is—I want it all. I want Chance Creek, I want land, and space and room to roam, I want a family, and I want to be… famous."

He laughed. She'd finally said it out loud. He realized he'd known it all along even though she'd never put it into words.

"I talked to Autumn, Fila and Camila today."

All women involved in the food business.

Cole nodded. That was a sensible thing to do.

"There could be a way for me to get what I want right here."

Hope blossomed within him. "Really?"

"Yeah. I'd still need a restaurant—"

He nearly let the cat out of the bag right then. "Okay," he managed to say instead.

"And we'd need somewhere to live."

"Yep." He'd start looking first thing.

"But most of all..." She faltered, but then rushed on. "I'd need your help, Cole."

"I'll help. I can renovate and install appliances..."

"With the kids." She spoke over him. "I want more than one. But I can't be at home with them. Not all the time."

Cole sat back, as if he'd had the wind knocked out of him. He thought about Jack slipping out the sliding glass door and the way he'd snapped at Sunshine for not watching him closely enough. "I don't know anything about kids."

"Neither do I."

"But you're a girl. It comes naturally."

"It would for you, too. You'll be their father."

Suddenly Cole felt like he was sliding underwater, firm ground nowhere to be found. "I need a job. Someone has to pay for all of this stuff." He was grasping at straws.

"We both need jobs. I don't think either of us would be happy without them."

"Then what are you asking?"

"That we share the child care."

Cole didn't know what to say to that. He'd never pictured himself spending his days with children. His father had never done that. Sure, Cole had tagged along after him as a kid—a lot. He stopped to consider that. Boys growing up on the ranches around here spent more time in the barns with the men than they did by their mother's side once they reached a certain age. But if Sunshine needed help right away, he'd have to start earlier than most—and rustle the girls as well as the boys. Could he do that?

He hadn't even figured out how to make a ranch profitable.

Cole scratched his head, more uncomfortable than he wanted to admit. "Can I think about it?"

"Of course." But Sunshine sounded sad.

"Give me one day to wrap my head around it." He leaned forward and snatched a kiss. "I love you. There's not a lot I wouldn't at least try."

"I know." Her hand caught his and held it. The tension in her body told him how important it was.

He wished he could agree to what she'd asked right now, but it was too big a question to guess at the answer.

And the truth was, he didn't know if he could be the man Sunshine wanted him to be.

"It's so good to be back in Chance Creek," Hannah Matheson said when she took Sunshine for a walk around the Double-Bar-K the next day. She'd driven herself over in the rental truck after Jake had come by and picked up Cole. She'd enjoyed the time alone. While the feeble sunshine left something to be desired this far into December, Sunshine felt like she'd been scrubbed clean. She'd done what she could do. The rest was up to Cole.

Cole hadn't talked much this morning, but he'd held her for a few minutes before they went downstairs, and kissed her softly. She was so grateful for his touch after their days apart, she'd almost cried. After leaving their things in yet another bedroom, Sunshine found herself with Hannah, whom she'd never met. A happy, confident blonde, Hannah's frank friendliness instantly charmed her. Spending the day with a stranger could be awkward, but she had the feeling they'd do fine.

"How long were you away at school?" She knew Hannah was attending college in Colorado, working on her veterinary degree. She and her husband had returned to Chance Creek for the holiday break.

"This is my second year into my bachelor's

degree. I've got so long to go." Hannah led the way toward a well-plowed lane where they could walk more easily. The sun was out but a cold wind whipped the ends of her hair around. Sunshine was grateful to be outside, but she figured their walk wouldn't be a long one.

"You sound energized, though. I'd expect you to be exhausted."

"All the younger students are." Hannah laughed. "You should have seen them at the end of exam week; they looked like they'd scaled Mt. Everest."

"But not you?" Sunshine matched her strides to Hannah's, her spirits rising the more they walked.

"I know how lucky I am to get to pursue my dream. I never thought I'd get the chance, you know? Now I am, thanks to Bella. Every morning I wake up and have to pinch myself all over again."

Sunshine had to grin at her exuberance. "And Jake's going to school, too?"

"Yes. I'm so proud of him. I uprooted him to Colorado, you know. It wasn't his idea." She laughed at the memory. "I wasn't sure how that cowboy was going to do at school, but he's showing me up."

"Really?" Hannah was right; Jake had looked like the quintessential cowboy in his rugged jacket, boots, jeans, work shirt and hat this morning. Blond like his brother, Rob, he was handsome and athletic, but he didn't look like a scholar.

"Uh-huh. Once he made up his mind to go, he didn't look back."

They paced along the snowy lane. Around them, the whole world was quiet, as if they were the only ones alive. Not a single bird flew nearby and no one was working outside, either.

"It's colder today," Sunshine said.

"I think we're due for a change in the weather soon. I heard we're going to get more snow."

Sunshine squinted up at the blue sky. Apart from a layer of haze, there wasn't a cloud in it. "Hard to believe."

"Wait until you wake up tomorrow."

Sunshine's phone rang and her heart fell. She knew without looking who it would be: Carl. Again. Didn't the man have anything else to do but drive her insane with his pestering?

She pulled the phone out of her pocket and answered it. "What now?"

"I need to know your answer," Carl said.

"And I need more time."

"How much time?"

Sunshine sighed and looked around her. The landscape held no answers. "One more day. Two at the most."

"You're killing me."

"That's the best I can do." She cut the call,

pocketed the phone and caught up with Hannah who had gone on ahead. They walked in silence for a few steps until they came to a fence surrounding one of the pastures. Finally Hannah spoke.

"So you're renovating a ranch and forming a rock band. Should I be hurt that I wasn't invited?"

Sunshine's mouth dropped open. "No one's supposed to know that!"

"No one does. Rose just told me this morning and she told me not to pass it on to anyone else. She said since I've got free time I should help you today at the house. Sounds like everyone else is pretty busy."

"You don't have to," Sunshine rushed to say.

"I want to," Hannah assured her. "I want to join your band, too. I play bass guitar, you know." She scanned the horizon like Sunshine had a minute ago. "But I am curious. Is Chance Creek where you want to be?"

"Yes," Sunshine said. "I mean, I think so. I mean, of course." She scrambled to make sense. "It's just—I want to do something big with my career. I have all these ideas. I think I can carry them out here…" She trailed off again.

"Can I give you some advice?" Hannah leaned against a fence post.

"Why not? Everyone else has." She smiled to show she saw the humor in the situation.

"Don't be a miserable wife. And don't be a miserable mother. Be real. Speak up about what you want and need."

"I've done that. I asked Cole to step up and help with the children when we have them. I told him I want both a family and a career and he's going to have to be part of that equation." Sunshine shoved her mittened hands in her pockets. The cold was beginning to penetrate her heavy jacket.

"What did Cole say?"

"He asked for time to think about it."

"Well, that's something."

"I guess I wish it didn't require thought."

"One plus about Chance Creek is that both of you would have a lot of support here. That's what I love about this town. Community isn't a word we give lip service to. It's real."

"I'm beginning to understand that," Sunshine said. "After all, everyone has opened their homes to us. I appreciate that. I guess we could have stayed at the ranch I bought."

"But that would have ruined the surprise. Besides, there will be paint fumes soon, right?"

"The painters are coming tomorrow to do the interior," Sunshine confirmed. "I'll have to stay out of it for a couple of days. The kitchen is still going to need a lot of work, but the rest of the place will be clean and painted."

"Cole's a lucky man," Hannah said, turning

back toward the house.

"I hope he realizes that."

"EVERYTHING'S CHANGING," JAKE said to Cole as they drove along the snowy roads into town. Once again Cole was directing someone to the restaurant he'd bought. He hoped Jake approved as much as the others had. If his conversation with Sunshine last night hadn't been weighing on his mind, the day would be just about perfect. The sky was a hazy blue, a brisk wind had cleared the cobwebs from his brain, and he was looking forward to getting his hands dirty and doing useful work in the company of a friend.

"In what way?"

"People aren't going to blindly eat what farmers and ranchers produce anymore. They're asking questions. They want the best they can get."

Cole nodded. He'd heard talk like that for a while. "People keep telling me not to get into beef."

"Yeah, the market's pretty saturated." Jake kept his eyes on the road. "But you know what we don't have around here?"

Cole perked up. That was exactly what he needed to figure out. "What?"

"Eggs. Free range eggs."

That wasn't what Cole expected to hear. "I don't know anything about chickens." He wasn't

THE COWBOY'S CHRISTMAS BRIDE

sure he wanted to know, either. Ranches were for beef, not eggs.

"You could learn, easy. I mean it, Cole. Have you seen what people pay for eggs raised without antibiotics? It's highway robbery."

Cole rubbed his face. He had noticed some high prices in the supermarkets. In fact, he'd made fun of those eggs. "What're they made of? Gold?" he'd asked Sunshine.

"At least the chickens who lay them aren't raised in gulags," Sunshine had retorted.

The memory made him nod. Free range. Sunshine couldn't object to that, could she? Well, maybe she would, being vegan and all, but she'd like it better than beef. He had a flash of her knitting tiny sweaters for the birds to wear in winter. Would they end up with thousands of pet chickens?

At least even pet chickens laid eggs.

"You really think there's a market for them?" he asked Jake.

"Hell, yeah. You'd do fine—if you can find a place. It's too bad you didn't get home a couple of weeks earlier. The old Jackson place west of town was for sale, but someone snapped it up right quick." Jake turned onto Main Street where Cole indicated. "This is a terrific location. You've done good, Cole."

As they got out and stretched their legs, Cole felt lighter than he had in days. Chicken farming.

Free-range chicken farming. That was an idea worth looking into along with the wind turbines. If Jake said there was a gap he could fill, he believed him. He was impressed with how entrepreneurial Jake was. He'd do his own due diligence of course, but gut told him it would check out.

Jake was right, though; he'd have to find a property.

Maybe it was time to start looking.

"If you decide to move forward with the egg idea, it's all about branding," Jake went on. "First you name the farm. Then you set up your business. You tell a story about your chickens and your eggs. What makes them so special? Tell the story to your customers and get them hooked so they keep coming back for more."

"You learn all that at school?"

"Some of it. The rest I know from experience."

"That is… brilliant," Cole said. "Chickens. I like it."

"Do you think Sunshine will like it, too?"

"God, I hope so."

"EMMA LARSON!" HANNAH suddenly cried, scaring Sunshine so badly she nearly dropped the bucket of cleaning supplies she was carrying into the bedroom. It was one of the rooms to be painted the following day and it needed a good scrubbing first.

"What about her?" Sunshine didn't recognize the name.

"She's wanted to open a bakery for years. She was almost ready to do it a while back. I remember she consulted with Regan Hall about how to get a loan, and I think she even bought a place but the deal fell through when she had to leave town to go help a member of her family. She's back now, though. I bumped into her at the grocery store a week or two ago, and she said she thought she was almost ready to try again."

Great. More competition, Sunshine thought.

"She might be a possible partner for you," Hannah went on.

"I'm not really so much into baking."

"Exactly. But Emma is. And she's into all that gluten-free kind of stuff. No one else does that in town. What if you worked together? With your vegan cooking and her gluten-free baked goods, you might draw a crowd from the surrounding areas." Hannah grew thoughtful. "Although now that I think about it, Emma isn't strictly gluten-free. She does a lot of regular baking too, which might not fit with what you want to do." She went back to work scrubbing the baseboards of the bedroom while Sunshine got to work on the trim around the windows.

"Actually, one thing I realized while I was traveling is that people are different," Sunshine said. "I know that sounds stupid, but it became clear that while I can eat a vegan diet and get plenty of variety in my food and be perfectly healthy, that's not true for everyone. At first I was kind of shocked by how much meat people eat around the world. After a while, I understood it. Different places, different ways of eating."

Hannah didn't say anything, but Sunshine sensed her curiosity. She knew the other woman was surprised to hear this take on things from her.

"I don't want to serve meat in my restaurant. I'm simply not comfortable with that. But if dairy products and eggs are produced in a humane way, well, maybe I can live with that."

Hannah set down her cleaning supplies, crossed the room and gave Sunshine a big hug.

"What was that for?" Sunshine laughed.

"Because I can tell that's a really big concession for you. And I know that you'll make absolutely sure that the eggs and milk used in anything sold in your restaurant will be sourced from farms that give a damn about the animals they keep. Which means people like me, who adore cheese, can eat it to my heart's content."

"You can eat it in thoughtful moderation, maybe," Sunshine corrected her, but as she turned back to cleaning, her heart soared. Hannah was right; lots of people wouldn't stop eating milk and egg products. She could help support a farmer who was committed to producing them humanely. "I'd love to meet Emma," she said.

"I'll set something up."

When Sunshine's phone rang, she almost didn't answer it, fearing yet another call from Carl, but when Kerri Olsen's name popped up, she clicked to accept it immediately. "Kerri!"

"Sunshine, I can't believe you're back!"

"I know. It's so good to hear from you."

"Listen, I can't talk long, but Mia stopped by my store today and she told me—"

"About my ranch and my rock band?" Sunshine said.

"How'd you know?" Kerri laughed. "Anyway, I'd like to help out. Can I come by later? I play bass guitar, by the way."

"Just like Hannah. We'd love to have you." She gave Kerri directions to the ranch and only realized when she hung up that she was smiling.

"See, you have to stay here. You have too many good friends to leave," Hannah said.

Sunshine thought she might be right.

COLE WAS RELIEVED to find Emma Larson at dinner that evening. Sunshine was too busy quizzing her new acquaintance about gluten-free baking to ask him if he was ready to be a stay-at-home dad. As much as he'd tried to puzzle it out in his mind during the day, he hadn't made much progress. The thing was, he liked tools and animals and hard work. He wasn't good at sitting around and he'd never held a baby in his life. Even if he wanted to spend his days like that, he wouldn't be any good at it. And the prospect struck him as…

Lonely.

After dinner, the women stayed in the kitchen to wash up. Cole wouldn't have minded cracking open a beer and watching some television, but he and Jake had to return to town.

Time for their stupid line-dancing lesson.

"Cole and I are off to do some Christmas shopping," Jake told Hannah. "Be back later."

"Get me something good!" She sent him off with a kiss.

Cole just nodded to Sunshine. She nodded back, immediately returning to her conversation with Emma. Aware he wasn't scoring any points for taking so damn long to make up his mind, Cole shrugged into his winter jacket. "Let's get this over with," he said to Jake.

When they arrived, light shone through the cracks around the windows they had newspapered over earlier. Cole climbed out of Jake's truck and was about to cross the sidewalk when he bumped into a man so bundled up he could barely see over the collar of his coat.

"Sorry about that." The man caught sight of Jake. "Hey, Jake. How's it going?"

"Hey, Carl. Good. You got plans for the holidays?"

Carl nodded. "The Coopers invited me to join them."

"Do you know Cole?" Jake introduced them. "Carl rents a place on the Cooper ranch."

"We haven't met, but I've heard of you." Carl chuckled. "You're a lucky man, I hope you know that."

"Lucky? How?" Cole asked.

Carl just shook his head. "You'll figure it out soon enough. Merry Christmas to both of you, if I don't see you again." He turned and hurried off down the sidewalk, disappearing into the door of the real estate office down the block.

"What was that all about?" Cole asked Jake.

"Hell if I know. He's right, though. You are lucky. You've got everything a man could want, don't you?"

Cole pondered that as he followed Jake into the restaurant. Was he making this all too difficult?

He didn't have time to sort it out during the next hour. Angelica Russell, a local dance instructor, had already arrived. Ethan and Jamie, who now possessed a key to the place, had let her in. She was just setting up the music when Cole and Jake walked in, a country tune with an up-tempo beat he recognized. Ethan, Jamie, Rob, Cab, Evan and Jake all stood around awkwardly, watching the young, beautiful woman prepare, and Cole was surprised to see Ned and Luke Matheson there as well.

"They offered to help. I told them if they help, they have to dance. I was surprised when they agreed, to be honest," Jake told him.

"Hate it when I screw up. Might as well get some extra practice," was all Ned would let on when Cole questioned him a few minutes later.

When Angelica told them she needed a bigger space cleared, they all jumped in to help move tools and boxes out of the way.

"You boys ready for this?" Angelica asked. She took a position in front of them. Dressed in jeans, a red plaid shirt layered over a white tank top, and a pair of battered boots, she was like any other young woman in these parts. Except Angelica was pretty enough to be a model. Cole expected the whole exercise to be awkward as hell with a hot young thing flirting with a bunch of married—or almost-married—men, but Angelica surprised him again when she turned out to be a no-nonsense teacher. She didn't flirt at all. Instead, she executed a series of steps, clapping out the rhythm as she went, then had them repeat it.

Their first attempt was downright pathetic. Cole just about managed to copy her, as did Jake and Ethan. Jamie and Cab crashed headlong, then spent the next few minutes blaming each other. Cole wasn't sure what Ned was doing—it wasn't dancing. Luke began to laugh the minute they started to move and couldn't seem to stop.

"Okay, okay," Angelica said. "Let's try that again."

So it went—with Angelica walking through each set of steps patiently and the men trying to copy them with varying degrees of success. Cole had to hand it to her—she had the patience of a saint, although she did finally separate Cab and Jamie before either of them landed a punch on the other.

As they went, she added each new series of steps to the old ones until an hour and a half later, they could do a complete song. The routine had lots of repetition, but enough variety that it wasn't dull. Cole felt like he'd actually accomplished something by the end of the lesson. At the very least, he was glad to find he didn't have two left feet.

Ethan looked at his watch. "Hell—I've got to get home."

"Chores?" Cole asked him.

"Arianna's bedtime." Ethan grinned sheepishly. "I give her a growly bear ride to bed every night. She doesn't sleep as well if I'm not there to do it."

"Lynn's the same," Jamie said, reaching for his coat. "Except she prefers a monkey ride. Sometimes it's off the hook. Claire hates it." He shrugged. "Thinks I'm going to drop her."

"We're not quite the hard-drinking crowd you used to know, huh?" Cab said to Cole, clapping him on the shoulder as he headed for the door. "Thanks, Angelica."

"See you all in a couple of days. Good work, guys!"

Cole and Jake waited for the others to leave and thanked Angelica again. On the ride home, Cole thought about what Cab had said. He was right; everyone had changed. They were the same rowdy cowboys they'd always been, but they'd grown up a bunch, too.

Their priorities had changed.

"Well, that wasn't as bad as I thought it might be," Jake drawled as he turned the truck homeward.

"No," Cole agreed. "It wasn't."

"YOU COULD STAY with us," Hannah said the next morning when she helped load their suitcases into the back of her truck, "but now that the rest of us have had our turn hosting you, Fila and Mia are clamoring for their turns. I hope you don't mind."

"Not at all," Sunshine said. It would be ungrateful to be anything but thankful that people actively wanted her to stay with them, but she was bone tired and still waiting to hear from Cole if he'd made up his mind. They'd gone to bed without saying much to each other again the night before, although Cole had kissed her soundly and stroked her hair before settling in to sleep. She sensed he was still deep in thought about the matter, and she had to appreciate that he hadn't simply stuck to his first knee-jerk reaction. Cole was a thoughtful man under all that testosterone.

Meanwhile, she had to make up her mind, too. She'd been waiting to hear what he had to say, but she couldn't put Carl off anymore and she had decided it wasn't fair to rest her decision to sell or keep the ranch on Cole. She needed to think this through herself.

Hannah helped Sunshine move her things into the small cabin Fila and Ned inhabited on the Double-Bar-K and then took her to her ranch so she could finish cleaning before the painters came in the afternoon.

"I wish I could stay to help," Hannah said. "Are you going to be okay out here by yourself?"

"Absolutely. To be honest, I'm craving a little time alone. I've got my cell phone—I'll be fine."

After Hannah drove away, the quiet settled in and soothed her jangled nerves, wrapping around her like a soft blanket. It began to snow, and—mesmerized—Sunshine moved through the house and out the door to the porch. She let the flakes fall on her face, shivering a little in the cold air. The hiss of the snow was the only sound and for the first time in nearly three years, Sunshine knew she was the only person for miles.

She let out a breath that she might have been holding since she boarded her original flight out from Chance Creek. She felt so much older now. Wiser, too.

At peace.

Sunshine nodded. She was at peace. She held her hands out and spun in a slow circle, letting the snow slip over her like a benediction. Of all the places in the world she'd traveled to, this was where she belonged. Life kept leading her here. She didn't know why. Maybe she never would.

It didn't matter.

She stopped her circling and peered out as far as the snow would let her see. Could she make this ranch her world? This town? These people?

She thought of all the women who'd come to help her over the previous week. Maybe she could.

Would she have to tailor her vision of her career? Probably, although her discussion with Emma last night had revealed a woman whose ambition nearly matched her own. Their ideas had bounced off each other until they'd hardly been able to breathe for the words spilling out of their mouths.

Had she found the kind of friend that made a place worthwhile?

Maybe she'd found a number of them.

She knew she'd found a husband she could love forever, despite his—she hesitated to call them *flaws*. She'd asked a lot of Cole by asking him to step into shoes society felt she should wear, but there were all kinds of compromises they could make. Even if he couldn't do as much as she wished he could, there were other options.

She remembered Autumn and the way she, Claire and Morgan swapped childcare. She remembered the way each of them had put their lives on hold to help her. She already had a community in place and she'd only been back in Chance Creek for a few days. What possibilities would the next few years unfold?

There was only one way to find out.

Sunshine pulled out her phone and found Carl's name in her contacts. A minute later he answered.

"Whitfield here."

"Carl, it's Sunshine."

To her surprise, he chuckled. "I know, I know—no deal, right?"

"That's right. How did you guess?"

"I should have known that first night. You were cleaning the place. Once a woman starts cleaning her home, she's not going to leave it."

"Well, that's sexist."

"I didn't mean it to be. Men do it too in their own way. It just usually involves tools and sheds."

It was her turn to chuckle. "Okay, I'll grant you that. I'm sorry. I know you're disappointed."

"I can't lie to you; I am. Can't get the girl until I have the house."

Sunshine went back inside and shut the door behind her. She crossed to the thermostat and turned up the heat. "Are you sure about that? Women kind of like to pick out their own homes."

There was a long silence on the other end of the phone. "Well, shit," Carl finally said. "I'm being an idiot, aren't I?"

"I'm not really sure." After all, she knew nothing about him—or his girl, whoever that might be.

"Sunshine, you might have stolen my ranch, but you just gave me a Christmas present I won't forget."

"Really?" Carl was kind of weird, but she thought she liked him.

"Really. Happy holidays to you and yours."

"You too—"

He was already gone.

Sunshine grabbed her cleaning supplies and moved into the family room, feeling happier than she'd been in a long time.

Chapter Eight

"I HAVEN'T TASTED anything this good since we left Turkmenistan," Cole said when he polished off a heaping plate of butter chicken nachos at Fila's restaurant at lunchtime.

"You have to try the Tikka Masala tacos," Ned said, pushing away his plate. "By the way—" He leaned closer. "This thing about keeping your restaurant a secret? It's for my protection as well as yours. I really shouldn't be helping the competition."

"Well, sounds like Fila and Camila have already been helping Sunshine brainstorm what to do next. I think you're in the clear."

"I generally am. Fila cuts me a lot of slack." The cowboy's fondness for his wife was all too evident. He kept glancing at the window behind the counter that separated the eating area from the kitchen where Fila and Camila were hard at work. "Good thing, too."

"I'd like to hear Fila's story sometime." Cole

had gotten bits and pieces about the way Fila had made her way back home from Afghanistan where she'd been held captive for over a decade. "Your wife sounds like a brave woman. And I can't believe what I heard about that firefight. A shootout in Chance Creek?" When the terrorists who'd captured Fila came after her, things had gotten deadly.

"With the local gun expert thousands of miles away. We could have used you that night." Ned looked grim.

"Sorry I wasn't there."

"You don't realize what's important until it becomes life or death."

"I've been trying to decide what's important," Cole heard himself say. He found it far easier to talk to Ned than he'd expected. He knew the cowboy. He'd grown up with the Mathesons and had spent plenty of time with all four of them over the years, but he didn't know Ned well. Still, it was hard to hold back what was on his mind.

"I kind of thought you had a plan. Marry Sunshine. Settle down?"

"My plan is beginning to take shape." He told Ned about the free-range egg idea. "The thing is…" He wasn't sure he could voice what Sunshine had asked.

Ned waited. He was patient, Cole would give him that.

"She wants my help—with our kids when we have them. Like, not just a little help. A lot."

Ned scratched his neck. "Welcome to the twenty-first century." He smiled wryly. "Remember all that hoopla about women having to do it all? I used to hear it on the radio out in the barn. Some woman would come on and talk about her career and her kids and her husband and how she couldn't do anything well enough. I used to think they were crazy. Swore I near about grabbed the phone once, called in one of those shows and said, 'Just pick something and do it, lady!'" He chuckled. "That would have gone over well, right?"

Cole nodded appreciatively. Many times he'd had a similar urge to sort out the callers on talk radio shows when he worked at the rifle range.

"But now I look around and it ain't just women—it's everyone. We're all trying to do everything. And we're competing with TV shows where the people are doing it perfectly. I reckon they got it worse in the city. At least out here we're too busy to care about what we look like for the most part. We know if we work with horses we're going to smell like manure. But even here—you seen what people are doing to their kitchens? I walked into a ranch house the other day and could have sworn I'd been teleported to Manhattan." Ned shook his head. "The world's gone nuts, man."

"You said a mouthful."

"But as far as babies and men and women? Maybe it's not so bad. My dad sure could have been a little softer around the edges."

Cole had heard the stories about Holt Matheson. "He raised you old-fashioned, huh?"

"Saw the back of his hand more than anything else. That's just the way he knew. Took a long time to sort things out and get to a better place. When my kid's born—" He broke off. "Hell. I just spilled the beans. No one knows about that."

Cole leaned forward. "Fila's pregnant?"

"Yep. Seven weeks."

"Congratulations." Cole reached across the table and shook his hand. "That's terrific news."

"Well, keep it to yourself; we're going to announce it on Christmas. You going to the Cruz ranch Christmas Eve?"

"Yeah, we're staying there."

"We'll tell everyone then." Ned grinned. "I'm going to be a dad. How's that for crazy?"

"You'll do a good job." Cole hesitated. "So what would you say if Fila asked you to step up and do a lot of the child care?"

"Fuck man, she didn't have to ask. I volunteered."

LATE THAT AFTERNOON, Sunshine took a taxi into town and joined both Fila and Camila for an early dinner. Finally she heard the full story of Fila's journey from a remote village in the mountains of Afghanistan back to the United States. Sunshine couldn't believe the courage it must have taken.

"We never went to Afghanistan," Sunshine told her. "We spent some time in Turkmenistan, but that's the closest we got."

"I'm glad you're both here now," Mia said. She eyed Sunshine speculatively. "You look different tonight. Is your morning sickness settling down?"

"No. Ugh." Sunshine still struggled from late morning through mid-afternoon. Then she became ravenous. "But I've sorted some stuff out that was on my mind." She couldn't wait to catch up to Cole tonight. Freed from worry about his choice, she felt so much better than she had in days. She wanted to reconnect with him. To start figuring out the future.

"You know, if you feel up to it, and if you have time, we could use some extra help during the next few weeks here at the restaurant." Fila flipped her long, dark braid over her shoulder.

"We've both been working overtime for months. We need to back off our hours," Camila put in. Like Fila, her hair was dark, but hers surrounded her face in wild curls. She was pretty and vivacious. Fila was calmer, but her eyes danced with fun.

They made a good team, Sunshine thought. She hoped she and Emma might become like them someday. They'd decided to wait until the Christmas craziness had died down to have another planning session.

"Would you consider coming on board? Only temporarily," Fila said. "We know you have plans for your own restaurant."

"That's going to take a while. I've spent my money on the ranch."

"But if you and Emma work together you'll figure out a way," Camila said.

"We'll see." She wasn't going to rush anything. She'd decided that for now she'd be content where she was.

"Can you keep a secret?" Fila said, leaning forward. "I heard about your pregnancy."

"I figured."

"I'm pregnant too. But shh. You two are the only ones who know except Ned."

"Oh, my goodness! Congratulations!" Sunshine wanted to hug her. "This is your first one, right? We'll be newbies together."

Mia laughed. "Welcome to the baby club, both of you. This is exciting!"

"So—will you come work for us?" Fila said.

Sunshine hesitated. "I'd love to—but you know I'm a vegan. I don't cook meat."

"We thought about that," Camila said. "What we really need is someone to help prep and to take over ordering supplies. You can be queen of the vegetables. We use a lot of them."

"And tortillas," Fila said. "We desperately need a tortilla queen. We only use handmade ones."

"I could do that," Sunshine said. It would get her hand back in the business and introduce her to local suppliers. She'd get as much out of it as she'd be putting in.

"Terrific," Camila said. She checked her watch. "We'd better get back to work."

"I'll walk over to Thayer's and catch a ride back to the Double-Bar-K with Mia," Sunshine said. "She's—"

The door opened and Carl walked in. "Oh," Camila said, cutting Sunshine off. "I'll take this order." She jumped up and moved behind the counter as Carl crossed to stand in front of it.

"Those two," Fila said with another toss of her head. "Someday they're actually going to date."

Sunshine eyed them curiously as she stood up and put on her coat. "Maybe sooner than you think."

AFTER A LONG day's work on the restaurant, and several hours spent helping Ned with his chores on the Double-Bar-K, the last thing Cole wanted to do was stumble through another dance class, but since all of his friends had been roped into it on account of him, Cole knew he couldn't bow out. This one went better than the last one had, but it was still hard to watch Ned dance and keep a straight face.

Afterward, they milled around by the door to the restaurant as they pulled on their coats.

"Did you hear about Carl?" Cab asked. "Rumor has it he's going after some ranch."

"I heard he put the bank on notice he might need a lot of cash to buy it outright," Jamie said.

Cole hid a smile. Small town living at its worst; no one should be talking about things like that, but somehow everyone knew.

"Who's he going after?"

"I have an idea, but I'm not at liberty to say," Cab told Cole. "But I sure as hell hope he doesn't get it."

"You've got something against Carl?"

"Nah, Carl's all right, but this particular owner shouldn't sell."

That was all Cab would say despite their attempts to get him to cough up more. Cole went home with an uneasy feeling in his gut. It was clear ranches were hard to come by in these parts. He didn't have a lot of cash left after purchasing the restaurant. He hated to think he might be forced to buy a small parcel of land instead.

Back at the house, he and Ned gathered with Fila and Sunshine in the living room for cocoa before heading upstairs. Ned turned on the television and surfed through the channels until he found a Christmas movie Cole had seen a half-dozen times. Still, with Sunshine next to him on the couch, and good friends close by, he relaxed, content. At some point he realized both Sunshine and Fila had fallen asleep watching the movie. He caught Ned's eye, grinned and raised his cup of cocoa. Ned raised his cup, too.

"Happy Holidays," Ned said.

"To you, too."

IT HAD BECOME so habitual to pack their things each morning, Sunshine did it automatically and was ready to move to Mia and Luke's cabin before breakfast the next day. Cole and Ned took care of transferring their luggage over, while Sunshine did her best to choke down a piece of toast and a glass of juice, fighting against the morning sickness that always hit her at breakfast time these days. She'd learned she had to power through it until the afternoon when it would subside.

She caught a ride to town with Fila, and made plans to meet up again with her later. Meanwhile, since the painters were hard at work at the ranch again today, she spent the day at Kerri's second-hand store. It was fun to help arrange new stock for sale and chat with Kerri in between customers. They finally had enough time to truly catch up, and Sunshine wondered why she'd ever been afraid she'd lost Kerri's friendship. They got along as well as they ever had.

"We have to do this more often," Sunshine said when it was time for Kerri to close up shop. They planned to eat a quick dinner out, then head over to the ranch to meet up with the other women for a practice session.

"Definitely. I'm so glad you're home." Kerri gave her a quick hug.

After dinner, they bundled up against the cold and headed to Kerri's truck. It took a long time for the vehicle to heat up as they drove the dark, quiet roads to Sunshine's ranch.

"Are you excited to see what the walls look like?"

"More than I can say."

When they finally let themselves into the house, Sunshine whooped with delight. "It's perfect. The painters did such a good job."

"If Claire uses them, you know they're good." Kerri joined her inside. They made their way from room to room, oohing and aahing over the colors in each of them. "The place looks classy and warm at the same time. Once you get furniture in here, it'll look great."

"Bella is going to send Evan on errands to-morrow morning and I've hired a handyman to move some of her old things here for now. I'll have enough furniture for a living room and bedroom. We'll put a table and chairs in the living room to eat at until the kitchen gets fixed up." She led the way to that room and sighed. "I didn't bother to have it painted because the whole room needs to be gutted. There wasn't time to put new cabinets or countertops in, let alone appliances and flooring. I'll have to do all that after Christmas."

"The rest of the house looks terrific."

"Some of it does," Sunshine agreed. "Enough so that Cole will get the idea."

A knock sounded on the door. Sunshine went to answer it and found Mia outside.

"Rock band time!" Mia said. "Can you help me unload my drums?"

"Of course." Sunshine grabbed her coat, pulled on her boots and struggled with Mia to get all the pieces of her borrowed drum set into the house. While Mia put it together, the rest of the women arrived. Bella and Autumn brought their guitars. Morgan came with her tambourine. Kerri and Hannah had their bases, and Rose was ready to sing, with Camila and Fila as back up. Claire arrived last, a portable keyboard under her arm.

"Let's get this party started," Mia cried, banging out a beat that made the rest of them cringe.

"Can't you turn that down?" Hannah asked.

"There's no volume on drums," Mia told her huffily.

"We're all going to be loud," Autumn said. "Is everyone plugged in who can plug in?"

"I guess we're going to find out the state of your wiring," Claire joked to Sunshine.

"I had the inspector check that out before I bought. The panel's been upgraded." She had to laugh at how knowledgeable she sounded. In truth, it was the inspector who'd thought to look. When he informed her of the results, she'd had to look up what it meant on the Internet.

"Let's go then. Has everyone been practicing?"

"I have," Claire said.

The rest of them mumbled.

"Oh, for heaven's sake," Mia said, thundering out another series of beats and ending with a clash of the cymbals. "I'll play really loud. The rest of you do your best."

Their first attempt was an utter failure. The second was little better. Autumn finally put a stop to the proceedings and went down the line, forcing each of them to play by themselves. She identified their errors, made them play the piece until they'd memorized their parts, and then they tried it again together.

"That almost sounded like Jingle Bells," Fila said.

"Almost," Morgan snorted.

"Let's do it again." Sunshine loved it. So what if they sucked? She was playing in a band with ten other women. She couldn't wait for Christmas Eve.

They practiced a few more times, then broke up for the evening, with plans to have another session the next morning.

"I wonder if the men have actually learned a dance," Bella said.

"I think it's unlikely," Hannah said.

"We'll see tomorrow night."

The crowd broke up and everyone left in their vehicles, leaving Sunshine and Mia to shut out the lights, turn down the heat and lock up. As Mia walked toward her truck, Sunshine paused and touched the front door of her house. "One more day," she whispered.

She hoped Cole would love the ranch as much as she loved him.

Chapter Nine

COLE WAS RELIEVED when Sunshine and Mia returned home. When Luke asked how their practice session had gone, Mia merely said, "Wouldn't you like to know?"

Cole didn't care about anything except getting Sunshine alone.

When they finally went upstairs to their room, however, she immediately headed for the bathroom. "I need a soak," she groaned. Cole didn't want to wait another minute, but she did look tired.

"I wouldn't mind company," she went on, unbuttoning her blouse and throwing him a come-hither look.

That was an invitation he wouldn't refuse. Cole grinned. "Light those candles," he said, referring to the decorative ones Mia had placed around their small bathroom.

"I don't know if we should. Those look fancy—"

"I'll buy her new ones." He tossed her a book of matches.

"If you say so."

Cole stripped off his clothes as quickly as he could and grabbed the fresh towels Mia had laid on the bed for them. He joined Sunshine in the bathroom and watched the water fill the tub. The little room looked like it had been added after the original construction of the house, and the tub wasn't fancy, but Cole didn't care. As long as he was with Sunshine, everything was fine.

Sunshine finished lighting the candles, turned and took him in. If he'd worried that time and closeness would diminish the rush between them, he'd been wrong. He knew Sunshine well, and her survey of his body was appreciative. Without a word she began to undress as the hot water sent billows of steam into the small room.

Her languorous movements were a slow torture. He wanted to touch her, but somehow he knew that she wanted to set the pace. That was fine with him. When she was finished undressing she stepped closer to him, placed her hands on his hips and knelt down before him, her fingertips tracing down his skin.

Cole shivered, then let out a breath as she took him into her mouth. With a groan, he braced his right hand on the counter, the fingers of his left tangling in Sunshine's hair. She started slowly, tracing the tip of him with her tongue, but when she slid him deep inside, the hot, wet heat of her mouth set every nerve in his body alight.

Cole had meant to seduce Sunshine tonight, but now he was putty in her hands. As she set up a slow, powerful rhythm, he could only try to hang on.

"Oh... God." It wasn't original, but he couldn't manage anything else. Her mouth teased him, taking him so close to the edge he had to brace himself not to end this before it had hardly begun. He felt like a sixteen-year-old, every touch brand new, but he was glad he wasn't a teenager, because he wanted to make love to Sunshine like a man.

Sunshine slid her tongue over him and aroused him even further. He was so hard he ached with wanting her. When he began to think he might black out if he didn't find a release soon, he gently pulled back, tugged Sunshine to her feet, turned her around and braced her hands on the counter.

Perfect.

Now he could see her reflected in the wide mirror, and he wanted to watch her as he made her come. Sliding one hand up to cup her breast, he reached down with the other between her legs. Just as he suspected, she was more than ready for him.

It was her turn to moan as he sampled both

delights, squeezing her breast gently, savoring the heft of it in his hand, using his thumb and forefinger to play with her nipple until it was as hard as he was. He set up a rhythm with his hand between her legs and soon Sunshine rocked against him, echoing that rhythm unconsciously. Cole loved the look of his hands on her body, and he loved watching her expressions as he teased her. When she panted his name—half a cry, half laughing, Cole gripped her hip, and pushed inside of her.

Sunshine cried out softly and bit her lip again. He knew she was trying to keep it down out of respect for Luke and Mia. Cole couldn't care less about anyone else; he was too far gone. He crushed Sunshine to him, thrust inside her again and kissed the back of her neck, her hair tickling his nose. Sunshine pushed back against him, her eyes closed and her expression so blissed out, Cole knew she felt as good as he did.

He'd meant to pace himself and drive into her with slow, steady strokes, but Cole lost control, thrust into her again and again, and Sunshine arched against him, her breasts slipping through his fingers as they rode the wave of his desire to crash-land together in an orgasm that shook both of them simultaneously.

By the time he'd pulsed out the last of his release, Sunshine had folded over to rest her forehead on her arms. She was shaking so hard that Cole became concerned. Was she…

Crying?

"Sunshine?" He pulled her upright, slid himself out of her and turned her around. "What's wrong?"

But she wasn't crying—she was laughing.

And she couldn't stop.

Cole watched her, bemused, but in short order he became uncomfortable. Was she laughing at him?

"What's so funny?"

"Us," she managed to say. "I don't know about you, but I was aiming for a long, drawn-out, passionate night. That took us what—five minutes?"

"We could do it again." Cole was affronted.

"Of course we'll do it again." Sunshine flung her arms around his neck. "I love the way we're always in sync. I love the way you make love to me. That was one of the best—"

Cole cut her off with a kiss. He knew exactly what she meant. Slow or fast, hard or soft, every time they touched each other was magic. He moved her toward the tub. "Better get in there before it gets cold." He steadied her as she stepped into the water and then joined her there. He sat down and pulled her into his lap as he sat back against the wall of the pleasantly deep tub. Locating the soap, he lathered up and began to wash her body, paying particular attention to her breasts. Sunshine's breathing hitched.

"Oh, that feels good." She lay back against him, relaxed and for a moment Cole knew true contentment. His eyes drifted closed as he explored Sunshine's body and he couldn't help smile. This was his definition of heaven.

He was well along to being ready for another round of lovemaking when Sunshine spoke again.

"Cole, about what I asked you…"

WHEN COLE STIFFENED behind her, his hands stopping mid-stroke, Sunshine knew she had his attention. She hadn't meant to spoil the mood, but things needed to be said and now was the time to say them.

"I've thought about that a lot," he said, his deep voice rumbling against her back.

"I know," she hurried to say. "I know that I was asking you a lot. I've realized I don't—"

"I'll do it."

Sunshine twisted around to look at him. "Really?"

"Really. There'll have to be compromises, though. If we're both working full time, we'll need help."

"Of course." She hadn't realized how much it would mean to her for Cole to say what he'd said. "But do you really mean it?"

"I just said I did." He chuckled. "Don't you

believe me?"

"Of course I do. It's just—"

"It's just nothing. It's what I want to do. There's something else we need to talk about, though."

"What's that?" Worry gripped her again. Cole sounded so serious.

"We need to set a date for our wedding. I was going to wait until Christmas morning to ask you when you wanted to get hitched, but I can't wait any longer. I'm ready to move ahead with our lives."

Sunshine couldn't wait either. Suddenly she wanted Cole—all of him—and not just between her legs but in her life, signed, sealed and delivered with Montana's stamp of approval on it. "When?"

"Whenever you want. How about on New Year's? We can throw together a wedding in a week, can't we?"

Sunshine didn't care if they could or not. "Yes. New Year's. We'll invite everyone. I'll ask Mia for help." She reached up and kissed him under his chin. He turned her back to her original position, lifted her up and settled her more firmly on his lap. It was obvious he was ready to make love to her again.

She was ready for him, too.

She lifted her hips and sank down again as he pushed inside. The water rippled with their movements and Sunshine sighed, knowing what bliss was to come. Once again, Cole made good use of his position to stroke her body until Sunshine was burning with desire. Cole thrust in and out of her slowly until he had her writhing against him, wanting more. Her position gave her no control over the situation, so all she could do was lie back and let Cole love her, which he did with a skill that brought her to an earth-shattering climax before too long. As he pulsed into her, his groans mingling with her cries, Sunshine knew she'd found the man she was made to spend her life with. Their lives would be complicated, but she didn't care; not as long as she had Cole.

"I GUESS THIS is as good as it gets," Cole said cheerfully as he and Luke prepared to leave the restaurant the next afternoon. The youngest Matheson son, Luke, was every inch a cowboy, and reveled in running the Double-Bar-K. He had offered to lend Cole a hand to finish up the last-minute details at the restaurant, and he'd brought his daughter, Pam, along so that Mia could finish preparations for the Christmas Eve celebrations.

Luke had managed to help a lot while Pam played with the toys he'd placed inside her portable playpen. Every twenty minutes or so, he lifted her out and carried her piggy back around the place to check things out. The little girl crowed with laughter every time he lifted her to his shoulders, using her tiny fingers to twist his short hair into reins which she used to guide him around. Cole had to laugh to see the cocky cowboy at the mercy of his daughter, but Luke bore it all with a sense of humor and good grace. "Can't raise a pushover," he said to Cole at one point. "I know what men are like. If I have anything to say about it, she's going to be one formidable lady."

"I think the place looks great," Luke said now. He pushed open the front door and let a swirl of cold air blow in. Still holding Pam in one arm, he picked up her portable playpen, hefted it through the opening, and set it down on the sidewalk outside.

Cole agreed. The place was clean, all traces of the former 80s décor gone. The floors looked great and the walls had been painted a warm modern tone that would give Sunshine a hint of the possibilities the place held. While it lacked tables and chairs, he knew she'd want to pick out those herself. The space was clean and open. He felt sure Sunshine would love it.

Cole stepped onto the sidewalk and locked the door. He gave the exterior a once-over and followed Luke to his truck. Before he could open the door and get in, however, his phone rang.

"Cole, it's Bella," the voice on the other end

said when he accepted the call. "You got a minute?"

"Sure." He got into the truck and fastened his seatbelt one handed. Luke got Pam into her car seat and went to start the engine.

"You've probably got all your Christmas shopping done for Sunshine, but if you're still looking for something, I have an idea."

"What is it?" He was pretty sure that nothing Bella could come up with could top the restaurant.

"Back when you two stayed with us, I showed her the animals in my shelter and she fell in love with one of the dogs. Duke's a mutt—a big yellow dog that's got some retriever in him and who knows what else—"

"I'll take him." Cole cut her off.

"But I haven't even—"

"If Sunshine wants a big, yellow dog, she's getting a big, yellow dog," Cole said. "It's a done deal." He remembered how he'd thought she might be cheating on him, and then he'd thought that she was trying to buy him a dog. Now he knew she'd been worried about juggling a career and kids.

"Well... great! How about I bring him by tomorrow? I can take him home again until you have a place to keep him."

"I appreciate that. We'll work that out as quickly as we can."

"See you tonight!"

"See you."

"You're getting a dog?" Luke asked as he pulled out into traffic.

"That's right."

"Now all you need is a ranch."

Exactly. But not a cattle ranch. A chicken and wind turbine ranch. Cole chuckled. Would all his friends think he was nuts?

Maybe he was—for Sunshine, for Chance Creek—for this whole crazy life he was building.

Pam squealed in the back seat.

"Yeah, honey—I know how you feel," Cole said.

"IT'S CHRISTMAS! IT'S Christmas, it's Christmas, it's Christmas!" Mia sang as she packed the food she'd prepared in covered dishes and stacked them in preparation to load in her truck.

"You love the holidays, don't you?" Sunshine said. It was obvious. Mia and Luke's cabin was decorated to the hilt and the petite brunette had been almost dancing around the kitchen for the last few hours.

"I adore them. People, food, celebrations— all of it. I'm so glad we decided to celebrate all together tonight."

Sunshine agreed. While they'd all spend to- morrow with their families, tonight they'd join together. The plan was for an early potluck dinner at the Cruz ranch and an informal secret Santa gift exchange. Each of them had pulled a name out of a hat and there'd been a lot of speculation about who had whom. Sunshine looked forward to the look on Ned Matheson's face when he saw the funny tie with horses on it she'd bought him. The women were supposed to play their song and the men were supposed to do their dance. Then the whole lot of them would load up their vehicles and go to church for the candlelight service. The evening sounded wonderful, although she had a few nervous pangs about performing. And really—everything was lovely now that she was engaged to Cole.

Cole, Luke and Pam came in, bringing a rush of cold air. Pam thrust her arms out toward Mia and she crossed the room to hug her baby girl.

"Just about ready?" Luke asked Mia.

"Let me change Pam and we'll go."

Twenty minutes later, they spilled through the front door of the Cruz ranch guest house to find the party already in full swing. In the kitchen, Autumn and some of the other women were setting out trays of food, dishes and silverware. Sunshine went to join them, helping to carry Mia's offerings. Without a kitchen to cook in, she hadn't been able to contribute, so she'd asked Cole to pick up several bottles of wine. Morgan handed her a corkscrew when she went looking for one and she got to work opening one of the best. She wouldn't be able to drink any; nor would several other women attending. Good thing she and Mia had picked up some non-alcoholic wine, as well.

With toddlers racing underfoot and grownups seated and standing anywhere they could find space, the occasion was certainly festive. There were faces Sunshine didn't know, members of her friends' families who had come to stay for the holidays, but there were others she recognized from when she lived in town before, including the Matheson boys' parents, Lisa and Holt. She had to smile, remembering the gruff old man who used to drop by Cole's rifle range. Rose grabbed her hand. "Help me pass around the appetizers."

Between making the rounds of the room, eating plateful after plateful of delicious food and laughing at the antics of the children, the time passed swiftly, until Ethan pulled out a cordless microphone, turned it on and tapped it, making everyone cover their ears.

"Howdy, folks," he said. "I know, I know—what has it come to that I need a microphone? I knew we'd have a rowdy bunch tonight, though." He was interrupted by cheers and catcalls. Ethan waved them down. "Find a seat if you can so we can get things started. We're going to begin with some announcements. Apparently a bunch of you have been busy. So let's start with babies." A murmur of interest ran around the room. "We've got several expecting mothers in the audience," Ethan went on.

Sunshine went cold as Cole moved to stand beside her. Had someone told Ethan her news? Was he going to announce it?

"The first is my own lovely wife, Autumn! We're due in June, and I can't wait."

A cheer went up from the crowd. Autumn blushed becomingly and patted her belly.

"Next is Morgan. Good job, Rob! Way to go!"

Everyone laughed. Morgan beamed. "We're due in May," she called.

"And now we have a new mother. Bella? Stand up—when are you due?"

"July," Bella called out, not bothering to get up from the plush sofa.

"And Fila is another first-time mom. Lots more Mathesons to terrorize the world, huh, boys?"

"You got that right," Holt Matheson called out.

"And before you ask, we're due in June, too," Ned said.

Sunshine couldn't believe how many babies were coming. She wished she'd told Cole so that they could announce theirs, too. But she was grateful no one had spilled the beans.

"And last, but certainly not least, Mia and

Luke!"

Luke kissed his wife. "We're due in May, as well. I bet we beat everyone!"

Cole slipped an arm around Sunshine. "Can't wait until we can announce a baby of ours is coming."

Sunshine sucked in a breath. She'd meant to keep her news a secret until the morning, but he'd caught her by surprise and his enthusiasm disarmed her. Cole turned to peer down at her. Sunshine met his gaze. She tried not to show her feelings, but her eyes stung with tears.

"Sunshine? Are you—?"

She nodded.

"You're pregnant?"

She nodded again, then realized his words had fallen into a quiet room. Ethan had covered the mic and turned to consult with Jamie about something, so the people who stood around Sunshine and Cole had definitely overheard what Cole said.

Cole lifted her off her feet into a crushing hug. "Holy cow, you're really pregnant?"

That caught Ethan's attention. He turned the mic on again. "What's that? We got another baby coming?"

"Sunshine's pregnant! We're pregnant!" Cole spun her around and she clung to him, her tears spilling over. She hadn't known how hard it was to keep her secret until she'd let it go, but as Cole crowed and kissed her again and again, joy filled her heart until she thought it would burst.

"Well, there you have it—another baby!" Ethan said.

Cole finally put her down and planted another kiss on her mouth. "When?"

"July," she managed to say. "Late July."

"July," Ethan echoed. "Anyone else have anything to confess?" When no one spoke up, he went on. "Well, in light of that last surprise announcement, I'm happy to be able to tell you this next bit of news. Cole and Sunshine have set a date—they're marrying in one week! Everyone free on New Year's? If not, clear your calendar!"

Cheers and whistles filled the room and Cole ducked down to kiss her again. In the ensuing chaos, Sunshine couldn't take her eyes off of Cole, even as people on all sides leaned in to give them their congratulations. It took a long time for the room to settle down again. Cole found her a space on one of the comfortable couches and sat next to her, holding her hand. All through the gift exchange, Sunshine found it hard to concentrate, even when she unwrapped a set of porcelain pony candlesticks from Jamie. Cole was going to be her husband. The father of her child. This was where she'd make her life.

It all felt so good.

"And now, I'm very excited to announce that we have a special performance in store for you.

Ladies—do you want to take the stage?"

"That's you." Cole kissed the top of her head. "Go get 'em."

Sunshine stood up, reluctant to relinquish their closeness, but as she joined her friends near the massive fireplace and picked up her instrument, her nervousness fell away. Everyone in the audience was a friend—new or old. Besides, surely they couldn't play any worse than the men could dance.

They plugged in, checked the tuning of their instruments and exchanged a *what the heck* shrug. Mia lifted her drumsticks in the air and hit them together four times. They launched into a somewhat ragged but rocking rendition of Jingle Bells and Sunshine wished she could take a photo of the grins that spread on every face in front of them.

She thought she mostly hit the right notes, but it didn't matter; what they lacked in talent they made up in enthusiasm and soon the entire room was singing the words along with Rose and the rest of them on stage. By the time the song was over, Sunshine's cheeks ached from smiling. They all erupted into cheers and she congratulated her friends, hugging each and every one of them as they placed their instruments back on their stands.

"Well, that was a hell of song, ladies. Thank you!" Ethan said into his microphone. "And now the moment we've all been waiting for. Gentlemen, it's our turn to take the stage."

Sunshine collapsed back onto the couch along with Claire and Autumn as the men trailed up to the front of the room. Ethan fooled around with his cell phone, which he'd set into a combination charging/speaker station. When he found what he wanted he tapped the screen and music started. He hurried to his place in the front row next to Cole. Beside him stood Jamie and Rob. Ned, Jake, Luke, Cab and Evan stood in a row behind them.

They began to dance.

Sunshine let out a whoop of appreciation and was quickly joined by Autumn and Claire. Fila shocked everyone with a ululating trill that cut through the pounding country beat of the song. Jamie lost his place on stage and nearly tripped Rob, but Rob grabbed his arm, shoved him into place and the dance went on.

They were almost as ragged as Sunshine and her friends had been when they'd played Jingle Bells, but that didn't diminish Sunshine's admiration for them. They stomped, turned and went heel to toe with their boots as if they were at a country hoe-down. When they spun around in synchronicity the women nearly fell off their seats clapping and cheering.

"Yeah!" Claire yelled. "That's what we like to see!"

Morgan gave her a high five.

Sunshine cheered along with the rest of them. As far as she was concerned, this was the best Christmas present she'd ever received. When the dance came to the end and the men stood in their final poses, she leapt off the couch, raced across the room and flung herself into Cole's arm's.

"Did you like that?" he said, lifting her up. She wrapped her legs around his waist.

"I loved it."

"Just wait until tomorrow. It only gets better from here."

Chapter Ten

BACK IN THE room where they'd spent their first night in Chance Creek, Cole woke the following morning to find Sunshine smiling at him.

"Hey, there," he said, running a hand over her silky hair. "Merry Christmas."

"Merry Christmas to you, too." She snuggled closer. "I love you."

"I love you, too. I've got some great surprises for you today."

"I've got some great surprises, too."

A knock sounded on their door. "Room service," Autumn trilled. "I'm leaving you a tray out here. Enjoy your morning!"

"Thank you," Sunshine called. "She is too sweet," she said to Cole. She slipped out of bed, wrapped a robe around her and padded to the door. Coming back with a tray, she set it on Cole's lap and climbed back under the covers.

"I could get used to this." Cole sat back

against the headboard and uncovered the plates on the tray. One plate was loaded with pancakes, sausage and hash browns. The other held fruit, a poppy-seed muffin and more hash browns. A delicate card reading "vegan" was attached to it. Sunshine beamed.

"This looks amazing." She settled in, too, spearing a strawberry with the fork Autumn had provided. "I guess we'd better not get too used to it, though. Next Christmas we'll be parents."

"I still can't wrap my head around that." Cole sawed through his stack of pancakes and took a bite.

"I can't, either. It was supposed to be one of your Christmas surprises this morning."

"That's okay. I—"

Another knock sounded on the door. "Incoming," Ethan said. "Hope you're decent."

Sunshine scrambled to tug the covers up. The door opened a crack and a big, yellow dog bounded in. He gave a bark and ran in a circle.

Sunshine squealed and scrambled back out of bed, her robe flapping around her. She ran to Duke and dropped to her knees. "Duke! Where'd you come from?"

"Surprise number one," Cole said. "Bella told me you liked him."

"Like him? I love him. Don't I, Duke? Don't I?" She slipped into a cooing doggy language only she and Duke understood. Cole finished his pancakes, glad his first gift had gone over so well.

When they'd finally finished eating, pulled on some clothes and taken Duke for a short walk, they thanked Autumn for breakfast and loaded the dog into their rental truck.

"How'd you know we needed to drive to see your present?" Sunshine asked him.

"I didn't. I'm taking you to see your other present."

"But you already gave me Duke."

He started the engine and pulled out into the lane. "Hold onto your hat, baby. We're just getting started."

SUNSHINE'S STOMACH FLUTTERED in anticipation all the way to town, not because she was excited to see her present—she'd already gotten so much—but because she couldn't wait to show Cole the ranch. Still, she wanted to enjoy every minute of today. She watched the country fall away and the buildings get closer together as they neared the center of town. She couldn't imagine what would be open this morning, so when he parked at the edge of a nearly empty Main Street, she didn't know what to expect.

Cole got out, came around to open her door and took her hand when she joined him on the sidewalk. He shut the truck's door behind her and led her to a storefront with newspaper covering the windows.

"Give me a sec." He went through the keys on his keyring, found what he was looking for and opened the door. "Come on in."

"What is this place?" Sunshine asked. She followed him in, blinked when he turned on the lights and gazed at the clean, empty, tastefully decorated space in front of them. It looked like—

She turned to Cole. "Is it—" She couldn't even put it into words. Could it be?

"It's yours. Your new restaurant." Cole tugged her further inside. "Do you like it?"

"Mine?" Sunshine couldn't believe her ears. "Are you sure?"

"Of course I'm sure. I bought and renovated it for you, didn't I?"

Astonishment welled up inside her. More than any words Cole could say to her, this proved his support of her dreams. As she moved around the large space taking in the craftsmanship of the floors and the pristine condition of the fittings, she could feel Cole's love for her in every inch of the place. "I can't believe it. Cole— it's wonderful!"

He scooped her up into a hug. "And we'll work things out with the baby."

"I know we will." She kissed him, arching into him. She didn't think he'd ever turned her on more.

He responded in kind and they made out like

teenagers until Sunshine pulled back. "As much as I'd like to ravish you right here, I need to show you your present."

"Can't it wait?" Cole growled, planting kiss after kiss on her neck.

"No." She pushed him away playfully, then caught his hand. "Come on. You're going to love it." But she had to take a last look around the restaurant. "I can't wait to get started."

"First things first," he said, tugging her toward the door. "You need to give me my gift, and then you need to ravish me. Unless those are the same things."

"Ha, not likely. I got you a proper gift." She followed him outside and watched him lock up again.

Cole sighed. "I was afraid of that."

She made him give her the truck keys. "Close your eyes," she said when they were seated inside. "No peeking."

He did so and blew her a kiss.

"Behave."

"Some Christmas this is turning out to be."

They teased each other until Sunshine turned into the rutted driveway that led to the ranch house. She'd gotten the driveway plowed so she was able to park close to the front door. "Keep them closed," she said. She killed the engine, hopped out and went to his side. Opening his door, she helped him take off his seatbelt and pulled him to stand outside. "Okay—now!"

Cole dropped his hands and gazed around. He took in the house and turned to gaze at the fields beyond. "I don't get it."

"It's a ranch! I bought you a ranch, you big dummy!" Sunshine nearly hopped up and down in her excitement. "It's ours!"

He scanned the property again. "The house or the whole thing?"

"The whole thing. Three hundred acres. Now, I know that's not big, but it's got a barn and—"

Cole whooped, picked her up and danced around with her. "A ranch! A whole damn ranch! Holy—"

"Cole!" She covered his mouth with her mittened hands, and then kissed him. "You're going to be a daddy. Clean up that potty mouth!"

"I love you," he said, letting her slide through his hands until they were face to face. "Sunshine Patterson, I love you, you know that?"

"I do," she said.

SEVEN DAYS LATER, Cole stood by the altar in the Chance Creek Reformed Church flanked by Ethan, Jamie, Rob and Cab. His suit's stiff lines made him distinctly uncomfortable. Still, he wanted to do this right—he was only going to do it once.

"Took you long enough," Rob muttered

from his left. "You really are a slow-poke, Cole."

"Yeah, who would have thought you'd be the last to marry," Cab said.

"Remember when Sunshine first came to Chance Creek? None of us had a serious girl-friend," Jamie said.

"Except me, and I lost her anyway. Thank God," Ethan said. They all nodded.

"Now here we are, every one of us tied down with a ball and chain," Rob said.

"Doesn't feel much like being tied down," Ethan said.

"Nope," Cab agreed.

"Life's pretty good—"

The music swelled and the door at the back of the church swung open. Autumn, Claire, Morgan and Rose, dressed in matching moss-green gowns, walked at a stately pace down the aisle and took their places across from the men. But when Sunshine stepped through on her father's arm in a dress that was all white and curves and billowing train, everything around him disappeared until they only thing he could see was the woman who was about to become his wife.

Cole realized that he'd gone without family for a long time and had been separated from his friends by half a world for nearly three years. Now he would get it all back. Friends, a home, a business, a wife—and a brand new family.

He swallowed against an unfamiliar feeling, desperate to keep control of his emotions, but when Sunshine met his gaze and smiled, he had to grin back. Some of the tightness in his chest loosened. He'd get through this without making an ass of himself.

He laced his fingers through hers the minute her father let her go and took his seat. Turning to face Reverend Halpern, he squeezed her hand and she squeezed back.

"Dearly beloved," the reverend started. The rest was a whirlwind of words and responses. He would remember to his dying day the way Sunshine looked at him when she repeated her vows, and as he stumbled through his he hoped she felt the same. It seemed an eternity before Halpern said the words he'd been waiting to hear, though.

"You may now kiss the bride."

Cole caught Sunshine in a tight embrace and kissed her thoroughly before he broke away to the accompaniment of cheers and laughter. They walked up the aisle, receiving everyone's congratulations before being bundled into the Town Car that was to take them to the Cruz ranch for the reception.

"This can't be real," he said to Sunshine as they drove. "It just can't be."

"Why not?"

"Because I have everything I ever wanted."

"Except chickens." She kept her face straight for only a moment. Cole had told her all about his plans after she'd given him the ranch. "You want chickens, don't you?"

"Free-range chickens. That okay with you?"

"Yes. As long as you understand they'll be the best-cared-for chickens ever."

"Of course." He reached down to pat her belly. "How's Junior?"

"Juniorette is doing just fine."

They wouldn't find out the sex of their baby for months. Cole was curious, but as much as he teased Sunshine, he would be happy no matter if they had a boy or a girl. After all, this was just the first one.

"Are you sure you're not going to miss having a honeymoon?" she asked coyly.

"No, I don't need to travel again any time soon. I'm looking forward to hunkering down in that sweet little house you bought me."

"Me, too."

"We've really done it, haven't we? Made this all work out."

"We have. I can't imagine what we'll get up to next."

"I can." He tugged her close and dropped a kiss on her lips. "Unfortunately not for hours and hours, though."

Epilogue

Eight Months Later

D ESPITE THE AIR conditioning, the heat
made Sunshine's loose cotton top stick to
her skin as she bent over the counter and packed
another vegan sandwich into its recyclable
container. In an hour or two the place would
begin to fill up with the breakfast crowd. Emma
was due in soon. This late in her pregnancy,
Sunshine only came in early mornings to make
the box lunches that had done so well for them.
It turned out that lots of people in Chance Creek
and the surrounding areas had food allergies that
made it difficult for them to eat out. Emma and
Sunshine had seen an opportunity and jumped
on it. Not only did they sell prepared meals to
individuals and families, along with their normal
restaurant and bakery fare, they also catered
corporate events when companies wanted to
make sure the food they served was appropriate
for a crowd with different dietary needs.

Sunshine had worked hard to develop a vegan menu that would appeal to the meat–and–potatoes crowd and it had worked to some extent. They made sure to attend every event in town that would allow them to give out free samples for people to try. They also held frequent tasting parties in the restaurant aimed at drawing a new crowd.

Sunshine was pleased with the outcome, although today she felt like her belly was in a vise.

Braxton Hicks contractions had started several weeks ago and increased in strength until it felt like every time she moved, one clenched around her middle like a band of steel. She heaved a sigh, packed another sandwich and slipped it in the refrigerated cases that lined one part of the bakery side of the building.

"Ouch." She braced a hand on the counter and pressed another one to her back.

"Everything okay?" Emma came in and hung up her purse on a hook. "You don't look so great."

"Thanks," Sunshine said dryly. "More Braxton Hicks. They never stop."

"Well, you should stop. Go home. I'll take it from here."

"I think I'll take you up on that." Suddenly she was too tired to think straight.

"Want me to call Cole?" Emma peered at her. "Or maybe your doctor?"

"No. I'm going to go home and take a nap. I might as well; this is my last day working."

"And about time." Emma came to give her a hug. "Don't worry; we'll hold down the fort until you're ready to come back." They had decided to close the restaurant for a month, but keep the bakery and packaged food side of the business open. Sunshine knew Emma would do just fine.

Another contraction squeezed her. "Thank you." She hugged Emma back. "Don't be a stranger, though. I'll be bored at home all by myself."

"Soak it up. You won't be bored again for a long, long time."

Sunshine waved good-bye to her, grabbed her purse and left the restaurant. Outside she climbed into the sky-blue GMC truck Cole had bought her so she could travel safely on the country roads to and from town. She started the engine and pulled out, grateful that work was over. She felt so heavy and her muscles ached and she hadn't been sleeping well these past few nights.

Out of town, she relaxed, letting out a breath. Emma was right; she should enjoy the next two weeks. Once the baby arrived—

Another contraction hit her, this one twice as hard and twice as long as any that had come before. Sunshine swerved, got control of the truck and pulled over, barely getting the truck into park before another contraction hit and a wave of wetness ran down her legs. She sucked in a surprised breath, but before she could react, yet another contraction squeezed her. She bent over, wanting to cry out with the slicing pain that wrenched through her, but no sound came.

This wasn't Braxton Hicks. This was labor, she thought wildly. She grabbed for her purse on the passenger seat in order to reach her phone, but when another contraction hit, she only succeeded in knocking it to the floor. She panted until the contraction passed, then tried to reach the phone again, but the bulk of her belly got in the way. She managed to unhook her seatbelt, push back the seat and crawl clumsily over the divider between it and the passenger side, but she was crouched there when the next contraction clamped down on her and Sunshine could only pant through it again, tears slipping down her face as she rode the wave of the pain.

She finally reached the phone, scooped it up and pawed at it until she found Cole in her contacts. As the phone rang, and the pain came again, she clutched at the back of the seat, still crouched on her knees, her mouth open in a silent scream. She'd never seen the county road so empty. As the phone rang on and on she realized just how alone she was. Never in her wildest dreams had she thought she'd face labor without Cole there.

Just as she was about to give up, Cole answered. "Sunshine?"

"Cole—" She broke off with another contraction and dropped the phone. She could hear him calling, "Sunshine? Where are you?" But there was no way she could answer until the squeezing stopped.

"In the truck. On the road," she finally cried. "Cole—"

"I'll be right there."

A pain clamped down on Sunshine and she shrieked with it, fighting against the urge to bear down and birth her child. She couldn't do it like this. Not here. Not without Cole.

But her body wasn't listening. Sunshine fought to remember the instructions she'd got in birthing class. Breathe. Something about breathing—"

Another contraction hit her and Sunshine held on for dear life, panting with the pain, trying to bend with it. That was better—a little. But the urge to push was so strong.

In a rush of clarity, Sunshine realized no matter what happened she was going to have the baby right here. As horror threatened to overwhelm her once more, a vision popped into her mind—a rough mud hut and women grouped around an open hearth. She'd seen all kinds of dwellings on her trip around the world and had met women who'd given birth in all kinds of circumstances. They'd lived to tell about it.

So could she.

At the next pause between her contractions, she clumsily bent down and slipped off her pregnancy panties. Thank goodness she was wearing a voluminous sundress. She didn't think she could have gotten off a pair of pants. She considered her surroundings but realized she had nowhere to go. The truck lacked a back seat and she wasn't going to give birth on the side of a highway.

Besides, she didn't have time to move.

The next contraction was stronger than all the others that had gone before it. Sunshine gave up trying to hold back.

She began to push.

"I DON'T KNOW where she is," Cole bellowed. "Somewhere between the restaurant and home. On the side of the road. And she's hurt!"

"Keep calm," Cab said. "I'm on my way. So are the paramedics. We'll find her. Don't get into an accident."

Cole tossed away his phone and stepped on the gas. He'd been out in the chicken house when Sunshine's call had come, which was why he hadn't heard it at first. Surrounded by free-range hens, he'd been fixing a feed trough, but when he'd answered the phone and heard Sunshine scream, he'd dropped everything and raced for his truck. Nausea crawled up his throat at the thought of Sunshine hurt. And if they lost the baby—

He drove faster, nearly veering off the road as he came around a curve.

He fought for control of the car, got it back and slowed down just a notch. Cab was right. No sense crashing now—he wouldn't be a help to anyone then. He heard sirens in the distance and stepped up his speed again. Where was Sunshine?

When he spotted her truck pulled diagonally off the road, Cole's heart lurched into his throat. He screeched to a stop, jammed the truck into park and barely remembered to shut it off before he raced across the road.

"Where is she?"

Cab caught his arm and stopped him from tackling the nearest first responder. "She's fine. She's pushing right now. Get around there and help—but first settle down."

Cole pushed Cab away, rushed around the truck and elbowed past a paramedic who was leaning in the passenger side. Sunshine clung to the back of the driver's seat, on her knees. The paramedics had draped the cab with as much protective pads as they could and the truck looked like a miniature hospital room, but Cole didn't care about any of that. "Sunshine? Are you okay?"

"She's doing great." The paramedic, a no-

nonsense blonde with her hair scraped into a bun, pushed into the truck beside him. "Remember to breathe, honey."

"You're almost there. Another push," someone else said. He looked past Sunshine to see another paramedic behind her, leaning in through the driver's side door.

"What do you mean, almost there?" he growled "Why aren't you taking her to the hospital?" What was wrong with these people? "Sunshine, honey—"

She sucked in a breath, clutched the back of the seat and bore down, emitting an animal-like groan Cole had never heard before.

"That's it. Keep going. Keep going—" the paramedic said.

The groan ended in a wail that stood the hairs on the back of Cole's neck on end. "Sunshine!"

Almost immediately she bore down again and it was all he could do to stand there while the paramedic behind Sunshine shouted out encouragement.

The truth finally hit him. Sunshine was giving birth—right now.

They weren't going to the hospital.

"Come on, Dad. Tell her to breathe. You know what to do," the paramedic coached him.

All the classes they'd taken together clicked into place. She was past early labor, past the transition. This was the real deal. Cole bent down and leaned into the truck so she could see him. "Come on, honey. You've got this. Focus on me."

Sunshine bore down again, emitting an animal keening that seemed to go on and on.

"All right. Nearly there. Nearly—"

There was a shout. "That's it, Sunshine. The head's out. One more push," the paramedic cried.

She pushed again, half groaning, half shrieking. Cole had never felt so helpless in his life. "You can do it," he chanted. "Come on, baby. You can do it."

"There you go," the paramedic said. There was a flurry of activity and a new sound.

Cole's heart stopped.

The tiny cry piped up again and slid into a wail.

Cole stared at Sunshine. She stared back.

"That's our baby," he told her. "Did you hear that? It's our baby."

Tears gathered in Sunshine's eyes. Cole surged forward and kissed her, ignoring the protests of the paramedic he pushed aside. Sunshine clung to him and he supported her weight as she bore down one last time.

"We've got the afterbirth. Get a gurney. Prepare an IV!" Cole lost track of the shouted commands around him.

He didn't care. Sunshine was alive. So was their child. Only when the paramedics lifted Sunshine from his arms, and Cab reached in to haul him out of the truck was he able to think about anything else. He staggered around the vehicle to find Sunshine lying on a gurney, covered by a blanket, their baby in her arms.

"Let's get mom and baby to the hospital," the paramedic said. "You can ride in the back if you like."

"You better believe I will."

Cole wasn't letting either of his girls out of his sight again.

"AFTER TRAVELING THE whole world, who would have thought I'd find my favorite vista right here at home?" Sunshine said to the other women who had joined her on the small back deck, their babies on their laps. Sienna suckled at Sunshine's breast. Autumn's son, Alexander, waved his arms as she held him. Morgan's son, Andrew, was fast asleep. Fila's son, Holtan, played in her lap, while Bella's daughter, Maria, gazed into her eyes.

After a month, the nightmares that had plagued Sunshine the first days after her birth experience were finally dwindling away, but she was recovering more slowly than she had planned and her restaurant would remain closed for another month. She was glad Emma was doing well with the bakery. Meanwhile, Cole already had more orders for his eggs than he could keep up with, so he was expanding his business again. He and Evan were still making plans for wind turvines, but they hadn't figured out the logistics yet. She was on the mend, but she wasn't ready to work yet. It was nice to know she didn't have to rush.

Something had shifted with Sienna's birth. Her goals hadn't changed, but her way of thinking about time had. Right now it was time to relax with her baby. Soon enough it would be time to reopen her restaurant, put out her cookbook and pursue fame.

"Did the doctors say anything at your last visit?" Mia asked her. She, too, held a baby—Veronica, her second daughter. Unlike Pam, Veronica sported a thatch of blond hair like her father.

"She said everything's fine. She said the fast delivery paired with the circumstances has just worn me out. As long as I rest, everything will be fine. There's no reason at all I can't have more children."

"That's good," Morgan said.

"I'm kind of glad for an excuse to take it slow," Sunshine admitted. "I didn't realize how hard I've pushed myself these past years. Sienna and I are going to relax for a while." She shifted in her seat and Sienna lost her breast. Her tiny face screwed up and she let out an angry wail.

"Good luck with that," Autumn said. "But yes—rest as much as you can. The restaurant will be there when you're ready."

"It really is a beautiful view," Fila said. "I could sit out here all day."

Sunshine agreed as she shifted Sienna to a better position and reached down to pat Duke's head. He'd turned out to be a loyal dog who was never far from her side. She, Sienna and Duke often spent much of the day out here. Cole had bought comfortable deck furniture and he always made sure she had everything she might need before he went out to work in the barns. He checked back on them as often as he could, too. Sometimes he took Sienna and held her while Sunshine napped. She'd wake to find him watching her, a fond smile on his face.

When the women left, Cole brought her dinner and sat beside her, a plate in each hand. "You look happy," he said. "Did you have a good visit?"

"I did. I love it—it's like being in a flock of babies when everyone comes over." They'd been doing so several times a week. She shifted Sienna into her bouncer seat on the deck in front of them. The baby gurgled, but settled in, almost asleep already.

"I'm glad you have company. But I also like it when they go home and I get you to myself."

"You don't think I'm lazy spending my days lounging while you work?"

"Are you kidding?" He speared a slice of melon off of her plate and ate it. "I love knowing exactly where you are. It makes my day to come visit my girls."

"It won't always be like this."

"That's okay. I'll love that, too."

Sunshine snuggled against his arm and popped a strawberry into her mouth. "You are the best husband ever, you know that?"

"I don't know about that, but I do know you are the best wife."

Be the first to know about Cora Seton's new releases! Sign up for her newsletter!

Other books in the Cowboys of Chance Creek Series:

The Cowboy Inherits a Bride (Volume 0)
The Cowboy's E-Mail Order Bride (Volume 1)
The Cowboy Wins a Bride (Volume 2)
The Cowboy Imports a Bride (Volume 3)
The Cowgirl Ropes a Billionaire (Volume 4)
The Sheriff Catches a Bride (Volume 5)
The Cowboy Lassos a Bride (Volume 6)
The Cowboy Rescues a Bride (Volume 7)
The Cowboy Earns a Bride (Volume 8)

Sign up for my newsletter HERE.
www.coraseton.com/sign-up-for-my-newsletter

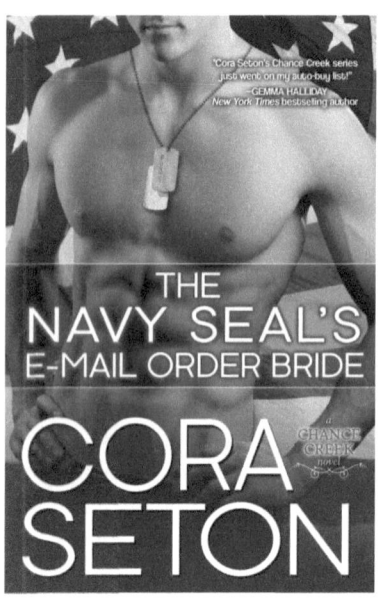

Read on for an excerpt of Volume 1 of
The Heroes of Chance Creek series –
The Navy SEAL's E-Mail Order Bride.

"BOYS," LIEUTENANT COMMANDER Mason
Hall said, "we're going home."

He sat back in his folding chair and waited
for a reaction from his brothers. The recreation
hall at Bagram Airfield was as busy as always with
men hunched over laptops, watching the wide-
screen television, or lounging in groups of three
or four shooting the breeze. His brothers—three
tall, broad shouldered men in uniform—stared
back at him from his computer screen, the feeds

from their four-way video conversation all relaying a similar reaction to his words.

Utter confusion.

"Home?" Austin was the first to speak. A Special Forces officer just a year younger than Mason, he was currently in Kabul.

"Home," Mason confirmed. "I got a letter from Great Aunt Heloise. Uncle Zeke passed away over the weekend without designating an heir. That means the ranch reverts back to her. She thinks we'll do a better job running it than Darren will." Darren, their first cousin, wasn't known for his responsible behavior and he hated ranching. Mason, on the other hand, loved it. He had missed the ranch, the cattle, the Montana sky and his family's home ever since they'd left it twelve years ago.

"She's giving Crescent Hall to us?" That was Zane, Austin's twin, a Marine currently in Kandahar. The excitement in his tone told Mason all he needed to know—Zane stilled loved the old place as much as he did. When Mason had gotten Heloise's letter, he'd had to read it more than once before he believed it. The Hall would belong to them once more—when he'd thought they'd lost it for good. Suddenly he'd felt like he could breathe fully again after so many years of holding in his anger and frustration over his uncle's behavior. The timing was perfect, too. He was due to ship stateside any day now. By April he'd be a civilian again.

Except it wasn't as easy as all that. Mason took a deep breath. "There are a few conditions."

Colt, his youngest brother, snorted. "Of course—we're talking about Heloise, aren't we? What's she up to this time?" He was an Air Force combat controller who had served both in Afghanistan and as part of the relief effort a few years back after the massive earthquake which devastated Haiti. He was currently back on United States soil in Florida, training with his unit.

Mason knew what he meant. Calling Heloise eccentric would be an understatement. In her eighties, she had definite opinions and brooked no opposition to her plans and schemes. She meant well, but as his father had always said, she was capable of leaving a swath of destruction in family affairs that rivaled Sherman's march to Atlanta.

"The first condition is that we have to stock the ranch with one hundred pair of cattle within twelve months of taking possession."

"We should be able to do that," Austin said.

"It's going to take some doing to get that ranch up and running again," Zane countered. "Zeke was already letting the place go years ago."

"You have something better to do than fix the place up when you get out?" Mason asked him. He hoped Zane understood the real question: was he in or out?

"I'm in; I'm just saying," Zane said.

Mason suppressed a smile. Zane always knew what he was thinking.

"Good luck with all that," Colt said.

"Thanks," Mason told him. He'd anticipated that inheriting the Hall wouldn't change Colt's mind about staying in the Air Force. He focused on the other two who were both already in the process of winding down their military careers. "If we're going to do this, it'll take a commitment. We're going to have to pool our funds and put our shoulders to the wheel for as long as it takes. Are you up for that?"

"I'll join you there as soon as I'm able to in June," Austin said. "It'll just be like another year in the service. I can handle that."

"I already said I'm in," Zane said. "I'll have boots on the ground in September."

Here's where it got tricky. "There's just one other thing," Mason said. "Aunt Heloise has one more requirement of each of us."

"What's that?" Austin asked when he didn't go on.

"She's worried about the lack of heirs on our side of the family. Darren has children. We don't."

"Plenty of time for that," Zane said. "We're still young, right?"

"Not according to Heloise." Mason decided

to get it over and done with. "She's decided that in order for us to inherit the Hall free and clear, we each have to be married within the year. One of us has to have a child."

Stunned silence met this announcement until Colt started to laugh. "Staying in the Air Force doesn't look so bad now, does it?"

"That means you, too," Mason said.

"What? Hold up, now." Colt was startled into soberness. "I won't even live on the ranch. Why do I have to get hitched?"

"Because Heloise says it's time to stop screwing around. And she controls the land. And you know Heloise."

"How are we going to get around that?" Austin asked.

"We're not." Mason got right to the point. "We're going to find ourselves some women and we're going to marry them."

"In Afghanistan?" Zane's tone made it clear what he thought about that idea.

Tension tightened Mason's jaw. He'd known this was going to be a messy conversation. "Online. I created an online personal ad for all of us. Each of us has a photo, a description and a reply address. A woman can get in touch with whichever of us she chooses and start a conversation. Just weed through your replies until you find the one you want."

"Are you out of your mind?" Zane peered at

him through the video screen.

"I don't see what you're upset about. I'm the one who has to have a child. None of you will be out of the service in time."

"Wait a minute—I thought you just got the letter from Heloise." As usual, Austin zeroed in on the inconsistency.

"The letter came about a week ago. I didn't want to get anyone's hopes up until I checked a few things out." Mason shifted in his seat. "Heloise said the place is in rougher shape than we thought. Sounds like Zeke sold off the last of his cattle last year. We're going to have to start from scratch, and we're going to have to move fast to meet her deadline—on both counts. I did all the leg work on the online ad. All you need to do is read some e-mails, look at some photos and pick one. How hard can that be?"

"I'm beginning to think there's a reason you've been single all these years, Straightshot," Austin said. Mason winced at the use of his nickname. The men in his unit had christened him with it during his early days in the service, but as Colt said when his brothers had first heard about it, it made perfect sense. The name had little to do with his accuracy with a rifle, and everything to do with his tendency to find the shortest route from here to done on any mission he was tasked with. Regardless of what obstacles stood in his way.

Colt snickered. "Told you two it was safer to stay in the military. Mason's Matchmaking Service. It has a ring to it. I guess you've found yourself a new career, Mase."

"Stow it." Mason tapped a finger on the table. "Just because I've put the ad up doesn't mean that any of you have to make contact with the women who write you. If it doesn't work, it doesn't work. But you need to marry within the year. If you don't find a wife for yourself, I'll find one for you."

"He would, too," Austin said to the others. "You know he would."

"When does the ad go live?" Zane asked.

"It went live five days ago. You've each got several hundred responses so far. I'll forward them to you as soon as we break the call."

Austin must have leaned toward his webcam because suddenly he filled the screen. "Several hundred?"

"That's right."

Colt's laughter rang out over the line.

"Don't know what you're finding so funny, Colton," Mason said in his best imitation of their late father's voice. "You've got several hundred responses, too."

"What? I told you I was staying…"

"Read through them and answer all the likely ones. I'll be in touch in a few days to check your progress." Mason cut the call.

★　★　★

REGAN ANDERSON WANTED a baby. Right now. Not five years from now. Not even next year.

Right now.

And since she'd just quit her stuffy loan officer job, moved out of her overpriced one bedroom New York City apartment, and completed all her preliminary appointments, she was going to get one via the modern technology of artificial insemination.

As she raced up the three flights of steps to her tiny new studio, she took the pins out of her severe updo and let her thick, auburn hair swirl around her shoulders. By the time she reached the door, she was breathing hard. Inside, she shut and locked it behind her, tossed her briefcase and blazer on the bed which took up the lion's share of the living space, and kicked off her high heels. Her blouse and pencil skirt came next, and thirty seconds later she was down to her skivvies.

Thank God.

She was done with Town and Country Bank. Done with originating loans for people who would scrape and slave away for the next thirty years just to cling to a lousy flat near a subway stop. She was done, done, done being a cog in the wheel of a financial system she couldn't stand to be a part of anymore.

She was starting a new business. Starting a

new life.

And she was starting a family, too.

Alone.

After years of looking for Mr. Right, she'd decided he simply didn't exist in New York City. So after several medical exams and consultations, she had scheduled her first round of artificial insemination for the end of April. She couldn't wait.

Meanwhile, she'd throw herself into the task of building her consulting business. She would make it her job to help non-profits assist regular people start new stores and services, buy homes that made sense, and manage their money so that they could get ahead. It might not be as lucrative as being a loan officer, but at least she'd be able to sleep at night.

She wasn't going to think about any of that right now, though. She'd survived her last day at work, survived her exit interview, survived her boss, Jack Richey, pretending to care that she was leaving. Now she was giving herself the weekend off. No work, no nothing—just forty-eight hours of rest and relaxation.

Having grabbed takeout from her favorite Thai restaurant on the way home, Regan spooned it out onto a plate and carried it to her bed. Lined with pillows, it doubled as her couch during waking hours. She sat cross-legged on top of the duvet and savored her food and her freedom. She had bought herself a nice bottle of wine to drink this weekend, figuring it might be her last for an awfully long time. She was all too aware her Chardonnay-sipping days were coming to an end. As soon as her weekend break from reality was over, she planned to spend the next ten months starting her business, while scrimping and saving every penny she could. She would have to move to a bigger apartment right before the baby was born, but given the cost of renting in the city, the temporary downgrade was worth it. She pushed all thoughts of business and the future out of her mind. Rest and relax—that was her job for now.

Two hours and two glasses of wine later, however, rest and relaxation was beginning to feel a lot like loneliness and boredom. In truth, she'd been fighting loneliness for months. She'd broken up with her last boyfriend before Christmas. Here it was March and she was still single. Two of her closest friends had gotten married and moved away in the past twelve months, Laurel to New Hampshire and Rita to New Jersey. They rarely saw each other now and when she'd jokingly mentioned the idea of going ahead and having a child without a husband the last time they'd gotten together, both women had scoffed.

"No way could I have gotten through this pregnancy without Ryan." Laurel ran a hand over her large belly. "I've felt awful the whole time."

"No way I'm going back to work." Rita's baby was six weeks old. "Thank God Alan brings in enough cash to see us through."

Regan decided not to tell them about her plans until the pregnancy was a done deal. She knew what she was getting into—she didn't need them to tell her how hard it might be. If there'd been any way for her to have a baby normally—with a man she loved—she'd have chosen that path in a heartbeat. But there didn't seem to be a man for her to love in New York. Unfortunately, keeping her secret meant it was hard to call either Rita or Laurel just to chat, and she needed someone to chat with tonight. As dusk descended on the city, Regan felt fear for the first time since making her decision to go ahead with having a child.

What if she'd made a mistake? What if her consultancy business failed? What if she became a welfare mother? What if she had to move back home?

When the thoughts and worries circling her mind grew overwhelming, she topped up her wine, opened up her laptop and clicked on a YouTube video of a cat stuck headfirst in a cereal box. Thank goodness she'd hooked up wi-fi the minute she secured the studio. Simultaneously scanning her Facebook feed, she read an update from an acquaintance named Susan who was exhibiting her art in one of the local galleries. She'd have to stop by this weekend.

She watched a couple more videos—the latest installment in a travel series she loved, and one about over-the-top weddings that made her sad. Determined to cheer up, she hopped onto Pinterest and added more images to her nursery pinboard. Sipping her wine, she checked the news, posted a question on the single parents' forum she frequented, checked her e-mail again, and then tapped a finger on the keys, wondering what to do next. The evening stretched out before her, vacant even of the work she normally took home to do over the weekend. She hadn't felt at such loose ends in years.

Pacing her tiny apartment didn't help. Nor did an attempt at unpacking more of her things. She had finished moving in just last night and boxes still lined one wall. She opened one to reveal books, took a look at her limited shelf space and packed them up again. A second box revealed her collection of vintage fans. No room for them here, either.

She stuck her iTouch into a docking station and turned up some tunes, then drained her glass, poured herself another, and flopped onto her bed. The wine was beginning to take effect—giving her a nice, soft, fuzzy feeling. It hadn't done away with her loneliness, but when she turned back to Facebook on her laptop, the images and YouTube links seemed funnier this time.

Heartened, she scrolled further down her feed until she spotted another post one of her friends had shared. It was an image of a handsome man standing ramrod straight in combat fatigues. *Hello.* He was cute. In fact, he looked like exactly the kind of man she'd always hoped she'd meet. He wasn't thin and arrogant like the up-and-coming Wall Street crowd, or paunchy and cynical like the upper-management men who hung around the bars near work. Instead he looked healthy, muscle-bound, clear-sighted, and vital. What was the post about? She clicked the link underneath it. Maybe there'd be more fantasy-fodder like this man wherever it took her.

There *was* more fantasy fodder. Regan wriggled happily. She had landed on a page that showcased four men. Brothers, she saw, looking more closely—two of them identical twins. Each one seemed to represent a different branch of the United States military. Were they models? Was this some kind of recruitment ploy?

Practical Wives Wanted read the heading at the top. Regan nearly spit out a sip of her wine. Wives Wanted? Practical ones? She considered the men again, then read more.

Looking for a change? the text went on. *Ready for a real challenge? Join four hardworking, clean living men and help bring our family's ranch back to life.*

Skills required—any or all of the following: Riding, roping, construction, animal care, roofing, farming, market gardening, cooking, cleaning, metalworking, small motor repair...

The list went on and on. Regan bit back at a laugh which quickly dissolved into giggles. Small engine repair? How very romantic. Was this supposed to be satire or was it real? It was certainly one of the most intriguing things she'd seen online in a long, long time.

Must be willing to commit to a man and the project. No weekends/no holidays/no sick days. Weaklings need not apply.

Regan snorted. It was beginning to sound like an employment ad. Good luck finding a woman to fill those conditions. She'd tried to find a suitable man for years and came up with Erik—the perennial mooch who'd finally admitted just before Christmas that he liked her old Village apartment more than he liked her. That's why she planned to get pregnant all by herself. There wasn't anyone worth marrying in the whole city. Probably the whole state. And if the men were all worthless, the women probably were, too. She reached for her wine without turning from the screen, missed, and nearly knocked over her glass. She tried again, secured the wine, drained the glass a third time and set it down again.

What she would give to find a real partner.

Someone strong, both physically and emotionally. An equal in intelligence and heart. A real man.

But those didn't exist.

If you're sick of wasting your time in a dead-end job, tired of tearing things down instead of building something up, or just ready to get your hands dirty with clean, honest work, write and tell us why you'd make a worthy wife for a man who has spent the last decade in uniform.

There wasn't much to laugh at in this paragraph. Regan read it again, then got up and wandered to the kitchen to top up her glass. She'd never seen a singles ad like this one. She could see why it was going viral. If it was real, these men were something special. Who wanted to do clean, honest work these days? What kind of man was selfless enough to serve in the military instead of sponging off their girlfriends? If she'd known there were guys like this in the world, she might not have been so quick to schedule the artificial insemination appointment.

She wouldn't cancel it, though, because these guys couldn't be for real, and she wasn't waiting another minute to start her family. She had dreamed of having children ever since she was a child herself and organized pretend schools in her backyard for the neighborhood little ones. Babies loved her. Toddlers thought she was the next best thing to teddy bears. Her co-workers at the bank had never appreciated her as much as the average five-year-old did.

Further down the page there were photographs of the ranch the brothers meant to bring back to life. The land was beautiful, if overgrown, but its toppled fences and sagging buildings were a testament to its neglect. The photograph of the main house caught her eye and kept her riveted, though. A large gothic structure, it could be beautiful with the proper care. She could see why these men would dedicate themselves to returning it to its former glory. She tried to imagine what it would be like to live on the ranch with one of them, and immediately her body craved an open sunny sky—the kind you were hard pressed to see in the city. She sunk into the daydream, picturing herself sitting on a back porch sipping lemonade while her cowboy worked and the baby napped. Her husband would have his shirt off while he chopped wood, or mended a fence or whatever it was ranchers did. At the end of the day they'd fall into bed and make love until morning.

Regan sighed. It was a wonderful daydream, but it had no bearing on her life. Disgruntled, she switched over to Netflix and set up a foreign film. She fetched the bottle of wine back to bed with her and leaned against her many pillows. She'd managed to hang her small flatscreen on the opposite wall. In an apartment this tiny, every piece of furniture needed to serve double-duty.

As the movie started, Regan found herself

composing messages to the military men in the Wife Wanted ad, in which she described herself as trim and petite, or lithe and strong, or horny and good-enough-looking to do the trick.

An hour later, when the film failed to hold her attention, she grabbed her laptop again. She pulled up the Wife Wanted page and reread it, keeping an eye on the foreign couple on the television screen who alternately argued and kissed.

Crazy what some people did. What was wrong with these men that they needed to advertise for wives instead of going out and meeting them like normal people?

She thought of the online dating sites she'd tried in the past. She'd had some awkward experiences, some horrible first dates, and finally one relationship that lasted for a couple of months before the man was transferred to Tucson and it fizzled out. It hadn't worked for her, but she supposed lots of people found love online these days. They might not advertise directly for spouses, but that was their ultimate intention, right? So maybe this ad wasn't all that unusual.

Most men who posted singles ads weren't as hot as these men were, though. Definitely not the ones she'd met. She poured herself another glass. A small twinge of her conscience told her she'd already had far too much wine for a single night.

To hell with that, Regan thought. As soon as she got pregnant she'd have to stay sober and sane for the next eighteen years. She wouldn't have a husband to trade off with—she'd always be the designated driver, the adult in charge, the sober, wise mother who made sure nothing bad ever happened to her child. Just this one last time she was allowed to blow off steam.

But even as she thought it, a twinge of fear wormed through her belly.

What if she wasn't good enough?

She stood up, strode the two steps to the kitchenette and made herself a bowl of popcorn. She drowned it in butter and salt, returned to the bed in time for the ending credits of the movie, and lined up *Pride and Prejudice* with Colin Firth. Time for comfort food and a comfort movie. *Pride and Prejudice* always did the trick when she felt blue. She checked the Wife Wanted page again on her laptop. If she was going to pick one of the men—which she wasn't—who would she choose?

Mason, the oldest, due to leave the Navy in a matter of weeks, drew her eye first. With his dark crew cut, hard jaw and uncompromising blue eyes he looked like the epitome of a military man. He stated his interests as ranching—of course—history, natural sciences and tactical operations, whatever the hell that was. That left her little more informed than before she'd read it, and she wondered what the man was really like. Did he read the newspaper in bed on Sunday mornings? Did he prefer lasagna or spaghetti? Would he listen to country music in his truck or talk radio? She stared at his photo, willing him to answer.

The next two brothers, Austin and Zane, were less fierce, but looked no less intelligent and determined. Still, they didn't draw her eye the way the way Mason did. Colt, the youngest, was blond with a grin she bet drew women like flies. That one was trouble, and she didn't need trouble.

She read Mason's description again and decided he was the leader of this endeavor. If she was going to pick one, it would be him.

But she wasn't going to pick one. She had given up all that. She'd made a promise to her imaginary child that she would not allow any chaos into its life. No dating until her baby wore a graduation gown, at the very least. She felt another twinge. Was she ready to give up men for nearly two decades? That was a long time.

It's worth it, she told herself. She had no doubt about her desire to be a mother. She had no doubt she'd be a great mom. She was smart, capable and had a good head on her shoulders. She was funny, silly and patient, too. She loved children.

She was just lousy with men.

But that didn't matter anymore. She pushed

the laptop aside and returned her attention to *Pride and Prejudice*, quickly falling into an old drinking game she and Laurel had devised one night that required taking a swig of wine each time one of the actresses lifted her eyebrows in polite surprise. When she finished the bottle, she headed to the tiny kitchenette to track down another one, trilling, "Jane! Elizabeth!" at the top of her voice along with Mrs. Bennett in the film. There was no more wine, so she switched to tequila.

By the time Elizabeth Bennett discovered the miracle of Mr. Darcy's palace-sized mansion, and decided she'd been too hasty in turning down his offer of marriage, Regan had decided she too needed to cast off her prejudices and find herself a man. A hot hunk of a military man. She grabbed the laptop, fumbled with the link that would let her leave Mason Hall a message and drafted a brilliant missive worthy of Jane Austen herself.

Dear Lt. Cmdr. Hall,

In her mind she pronounced lieutenant with an "f" like the Brits in the movie onscreen.

It is a truth universally acknowledged, that a single man in possession of a good ranch, must be in want of a wife. Furthermore, it must be self-evident that the wife in question should possess certain qualities numbering amongst them riding, roping, construction, roofing, farming, market gardening, cooking, cleaning, metalworking, animal care, and—most importantly, by Heaven—small motor repair.

Seeing as I am in possession of all these qualities, not to mention many others you can only have left out through unavoidable oversight or sheer obtuseness—such as glassblowing, cheesemaking, towel origami, heraldry, hovercraft piloting, and an uncanny sense of what cats are thinking—I feel almost forced to catapult myself into your purview.

You will see from my photograph that I am most eminently and majestically suitable for your wife.

She inserted a digital photo of her foot.

In fact, one might wonder why such a paragon of virtue such as I should deign to answer such a peculiar advertisement. The truth is, sir, that I long for adventure. To get my hands dirty with clean, hard work. To build something up instead of tearing it down.

In short, you are really hot. I'd like to lick you.

Yours,
Regan Anderson

On screen, Elizabeth Bennett lifted an eyebrow. Regan knocked back another shot of Jose Cuervo and passed out.

End of Excerpt

The Cowboys of Chance Creek Series:

The Cowboy Inherits a Bride (Volume 0)
The Cowboy's E-Mail Order Bride (Volume 1)
The Cowboy Wins a Bride (Volume 2)
The Cowboy Imports a Bride (Volume 3)
The Cowgirl Ropes a Billionaire (Volume 4)
The Sheriff Catches a Bride (Volume 5)
The Cowboy Lassos a Bride (Volume 6)
The Cowboy Rescues a Bride (Volume 7)
The Cowboy Earns a Bride (Volume 8)
The Cowboy's Christmas Bride (Volume 9)

The Heroes of Chance Creek Series:

The Navy SEAL's E-Mail Order Bride (Volume 1)
The Soldier's E-Mail Order Bride (Volume 2)
The Marine's E-Mail Order Bride (Volume 3)
The Navy SEAL's Christmas Bride (Volume 4)
The Airman's E-Mail Order Bride (Volume 5)

The SEALs of Chance Creek Series:

A SEAL's Oath
A SEAL's Vow
A SEAL's Pledge
A SEAL's Consent

About the Author

Cora Seton loves cowboys, country life, gardening, bike-riding, and lazing around with a good book. Mother of four, wife to a computer programmer/ eco-farmer, she ditched her California lifestyle nine years ago and moved to a remote logging town in northwestern British Columbia. Like the characters in her novels, Cora enjoys old-fashioned pursuits and modern technology, spending mornings transforming an ordinary one-acre lot into a paradise of orchards, berry bushes and market gardens, and afternoons writing the latest Chance Creek romance novel on her iPad mini. Visit www.coraseton.com to read about new releases and learn about contests and other events!

Blog: www.coraseton.com

Facebook:

www.facebook.com/coraseton

Twitter:

www.twitter.com/coraseton

Newsletter:

www.coraseton.com/sign-up-for-my-newsletter